White City
Book One / Spirit Gates Trilogy
By
Kenneth Trimble

First Printing

Dog Dujour Studio has allowed this work to remain exactly as the author intended, verbatim, without editorial input.

ISBN: 978-0-615-25358-9
PUBLISHED BY DOG DUJOUR STUDIO
www.stores.lulu.com/dogdujour
SALT LAKE CITY

Printed in United States of America

Chapter One

In the Future

December

December isn't cold everywhere.

It's funny, the human race. We freeze to death in the cold, but we never could colonize the warmer regions in a civilized manner. Wood rots in humidity and warmth too fast to keep up with, metal structures rust in moist climates, most annoying of all bugs bite, and there are so many bugs where it is warm and humid. So it seems that we went the hard route to civilized building. We colonized the cooler regions first, building things, experimenting, creating.

Harvey's family was wonderfully wealthy, and very large. Harvey, himself, was considered one of the poorer. He was a bastard, an unplanned child.

His father had many a mistress besides having a wife. Harvey's mother didn't even rank as a mistress. She was a Cajun woman who met a tall white tourist in New Orleans during Mardi Gras. She had been a momentary distraction during one of the most famous weeklong parties around.

Harvey had grown up never knowing who his father was. Interestingly enough, Harvey had never even been interested in finding out who his father had been. His father had mistakenly sought him out from beyond the grave.

Harvey had the media to thank, amongst quite a number of refined scientific tests, for the discovery that made him wealthy. He even had a few greedy half brothers and sisters to thank. The ones who thought they could clip out the children of his sires many mistresses were originally the ones who made a big fuss about the wording in the will.

The will was point blank, and probably a little too simple. It stated, "My children will receive equal portions of inheritance." Not a cent was left to wives mistresses and hookers.

Harvey's father had been around the block a few times more than the normal super wealthy playboy. His funeral became a media circus.

Harvey went in for blood tests along with billions of others as if it were a lottery. He, and over three thousand others were suddenly part of the wealthiest family on the planet.

There was one weird stipulation he had to live with. In order to inherit, the children had to sign an agreement to live in White City for the remainder of their lives, and anyone they left their wealth to would have to sign the same agreement.

The Legitimate children weren't too happy about the testing going on in regard to the inheritance. Most of them were pampered and very spoiled.

After it was done, it was discovered that family didn't mean much there anyway. Many of the mothers became penniless and homeless in a day. The lucky ones found a child of theirs to care for them.

Another minor stipulation was the use of the family surname. It had to be Tomm, regardless of married status. Anyone who wanted the fortune was required to take the family name and keep it for the remainder of his or her life.

It didn't bother Harvey one bit. He was a *Tomm* in many ways anyway. The name was sort of a personal joke. This new name took he and his mother out of the swamp to the finest city in the world, "The World Capitol!" White City,

Tomm City, and December in White City were very warm.

White City wasn't just a name. The city was white. It floated off the pacific coast directly on the equatorial line. It was white because of the material that it was made from. It was made of salt. Not just any salt though, but hardened salt.

Years ago an inventor had stumbled across a chemical formula that when applied to salt crystals made them the hardest substance known to man. There was a counter formula, of course, but it was never revealed.

Most people assumed that the chemical used to produce hard salt was extremely toxic since it was never revealed to the general public, and it seemed to only be used by little crab shaped machines named builders and cleaners that scoured White City, keeping the place tidy and clean.

Because the city was made of salt, which could be clear or brilliant white, and because the stuff was so incredibly strong yet light weight the city itself was like no other. The architecture was astounding, and many buildings and features were otherworldly, and would have been impossible to construct with any other materials available on earth.

Houses like Harvey's, which faced the ocean, were constructed as part of the weather shield system that protected the island city from heavy winds and tidal waves. They were not flat but leaned out over the ocean at an angle intended to push wind and water down when the weather was bad. They were stacked to make a very high wall that no waves would overcome. The rest of the city was domed over with crystal clear glass salt. It was seamless and kept the place wind free. The ventilation system, however kept a constant breeze flowing.

The plants were planted and maintained by the builders and cleaners. Just like the rest of the city. The little crab like machines cleaned anything not in their plan for the city out and away. The result was that the place had vistas and views that took the breath away. It was the perfect combination of science and nature.

Harvey stood on his balcony overlooking the ocean through his dark Cajun eyes.

"*Funny,*" he thought, "*Here I am in this paradise with everything I thought I could ever want, and I miss my dirty little shack in the swamps.*" He even missed the grime that used to permeate his skin and stick under his fingernails. He missed his pitted complexion.

"*Grandfather,*" he thought, "*I would have loved to meet the man.*"

Harvey felt a bit mystified by the view he had. It was sort of like déjà vu for a moment, because everything felt so familiar, everything from the hovercraft that flew by, the woman inside it bobbing her head up and down on the man's dick. The man taking in the scenery while his girl friend made him twitch with pleasure, to the pretty tropical birds that twittered past looking for fresh fruit or bugs to give to their young.

Harvey had grown up in a warm climate, so the salty humid air didn't even faze him. He loved it usually, but it was getting close to Christmas, and he remembered his five-year stay in Chicago. Since his love affair there with a now dead lover, he felt a strange need for snow in December. The time he had spent there had been enchanting, and it had been nice feeling, in many ways, free of his strange and distant relatives who squabbled amongst one another home in White City.

He and his man had spent weeks snuggling away the cold together, amongst other things. Then the cancer

had come and Harvey had found himself
alone and without love.

He had come home to his mom. She was
always there for him. She always had
been.

Harvey could smell a storm
approaching from out on the ocean. The
smell brought with it a yearning to do
something with his life. He needed a
purpose. In his head he imagined this
indestructible city falling down around
him just so he could rebuild it. Maybe
even find help rebuilding it with the
right man, Mr. Right.

Harvey's grandfather, John Tomm, had
been an inventor. He was probably one
of the more notable inventors in
history. What he did with his mind had
wrought just as much change to the
human race as the light bulb. Little
was known about the actual man. He
hadn't been able to enjoy much of his
wealth. It was known that his name
hadn't started out John Tomm. It had
started out, Juan Antonio. Where John
came from is obvious, but the Tomm was
a mystery. His father whom he had never
met boasted in diaries that he knew,
but he'd kept it a secret.

Chapter Two

Past and Present

Meet Juan "Sue, Such a Bitch"

"Juan?" He was stirred from his dinner and his secret thoughts by his wife's antagonistic voice. "How is your steak?"

"It's wonderful dear." He managed. He could hardly take his eyes off of their target.

Juan had grown up in a tight religious family. He went to church when it was time, and was mindful of his deeds, and tried to be mindful of his thoughts, but they so did like to slip into dark and forbidden corners.

He had met Sue at college. She was everything his mother had dreamed of in a daughter. Juan had married her for his mother more than himself. Still he was faithful, and quite dutiful, although he didn't find the woman even remotely attractive. Luckily she had always had strange ideas about sex, and hadn't demanded much from him until lately.

She wanted a child more than anything, and that meant performance. Juan had been on a strict sexual schedule, and it had worked. Sue had conceived. Juan was still on his best behavior though. His wife was a politician, a damned good one. She was definitely going places, and with so many political opponents looking and waiting for Sue to make a mistake, there were always appearances to keep up.

"Have you invented anything?" The lilt in her voice was mocking. Juan knew she couldn't resist mocking him for too long. His career was a failure. Everything he had tried since he met her had been a failure.

"No Sue, I haven't." She was risking a public fight. Testing his limits. He blushed a little at the antagonism, but resumed his earlier thoughts. Juan had a secret.

"I didn't think so." She rambled at the edge of his attention. "Would you like me to set some money aside for you love? Perhaps you need more funding."

Juan grew a little redder. She regularly attacked his pride with the fact that she made more than enough money to support them both. He noted it, and looked at the gentleman seated directly behind her. The man had entered a few minutes earlier, and Juan couldn't help but notice the tight pants, the way they had clung to the shape of his buttocks as he walked past to be seated. If his wife could see under the table at the large throbbing bulge in Juan's Sunday slacks she would have put two and two together, but she was way to pleased with her game at the moment.

The man Juan was looking at looked Italian, dark hair and eyes, incredibly hairy forearms and a strong build. At first Juan had pretended not to look, but the other man hadn't. It had started with a little twinkle in his eye, then the man moved his sitting position spreading his legs, and positioning himself in such a way that Juan had a good look at his groin where the slacks were pulled around what appeared to be a rather large piece of equipment. The man smiled, and when no one was looking reached down into his trousers and while looking right into Juan's eyes adjusted his package in a most arousing fashion.

Juan gulped down a lump in his throat, and wished he could adjust himself because he was terribly uncomfortable.

"You know, I think Bernard or Sebastian are good names for a boy." Sue said with a little bit of an

obvious push to her voice. It
definitely snapped Juan out of it.

"Bernard?" Juan said a bit
surprised. He realized he had to escape
from the situation or he would say
something he would regret. "Could you
excuse me for a moment?" He said to his
wife while standing. "I'm going to the
men's room."

"Why of course dear." She
antagonized further, happy with her
ability to get to the man.

Juan leaned against the counter as
he splashed cool water on his face.

"Bitch!" He said as the door opened.
He looked up and saw through the mirror
that it was the handsome Italian who
had entered. Juan smiled a full-toothed
smile, despite his anger. He had an
idea of what this man was up too. The
man smiled back. Juan watched through
the mirror as the man unzipped his
slacks and pulled out his dick long
before he reached the urinals. Juan's
hands began to shake. He knew it had
been for his benefit and he stared into
the mirror at the totally hard piece of
meat between the man's legs until the
man turned away from him to face the
urinals. The man looked down at his own
dick for a moment then turned his head
so he could give an inviting look to
Juan.

Juan had never done anything like this before.

"He had dreamed about other men for as long as he could remember, and then there was Sue."

That thought threw him over the edge. He was shaking like crazy as he turned around and approached the urinal next to the man. There were no other men in the rest room so they didn't have to worry about being seen. Juan was shaking so bad he had a difficult time unzipping his pants and pulling out his own very erect penis.

"Whoa." The other man whispered as he looked at what Juan had to offer.

Juan was busy himself taking in every visual inch. The Italian's balls were bigger than his own, and his dick was enormous, but not so long as Juan's own bulging masterpiece.

"The restaurant is slow, don't worry." The man said, noticing the nervous glance Juan gave the door. Besides, I own the place and I had a feeling about you. A server is watching the door, and if anyone approaches he'll warn us before they enter."

Juan relaxed as the man reached for him, and took hold of Juan's thick hard on. Before Juan could pull away the man had knelt and his mouth was over the entire expanse of it. Juan shuddered with the pleasure. His wife would never, and even if she did he would be left with his fantasies, eyes closed. Here he stood with his dick in a man's mouth, eyes wide, and nothing he could fantasize about would compare. He shuddered as his climax neared. His hands immediately stopped the man. He didn't want to cum yet. The man knew and carefully removed his mouth without brushing his lips against any of the sensitive skin, leaving the expanse of Juan's cock soaking wet and throbbing.

"Make love to me." The man said as he stood and walked to the sink and countertop. He dropped his pants all the way, and shook one foot loose from them, then sat on the counter and lifted his legs so that Juan could see his pink anus muscles twitching. Juan unbuttoned his trousers and let them drop to his ankles, and proceeded to unbutton his white shirt letting his hairy chest come free. His dick was so wet with saliva from the man's mouth that all he had to do was press the end of his cock lightly against the man's hole and it slipped easily in.

The Italian groaned and pulled Juan to him fully with his large strong hands.

Juan was still close and didn't thrust, instead he made busy unbuttoning the man's shirt. His dick throbbed in time with his heart as he

took in the vision of the man's massive
hair covered chest and trim furry
belly.

The Italian pulled Juan into him so
that their chests were touching and
kissed him furiously, his mustache and
the hair on his chest tickled just
right.

"Take your time Mr. The place is
empty except for you, your wife and
myself. We have time."

Juan rolled his eyes back a little
and rubbed his bearded face into the
Italian's ear.

"What's your name?" He whispered as
he kissed the man's lobe.

"Tomm." Came the breathy response as
Juan began to thrust slowly. The man's
ass felt so warm and soft around his
penis. He had never experienced a
sensation like this.

Not like the loose fleshy wet of his
wife's unkempt vagina.

"What will I call you?" Tomm asked.

"J…" He hesitated. A little lie
would be okay. "John." He whispered as
he began picking up the pace of his
lovemaking. His kisses fell hot upon
Tomm's face, and when Tomm introduced
his tongue to the kiss Juan was
thrilled to the point of climax.

"Cum inside me John." Tomm whispered
through the panting. "I want a part of

you to stay with me for the next day,
even when you've gone."

Tomm came in the same moment from
the friction of the hair on Juan's
belly against his dick, and as the hot
fluid filled his ass his own hot semen
shot up between them both in long ropey
jets wetting their chest hair, mixing
with their sweat.

Juan held his dick in deep and
kissed Tomm just as deep, then leaned
back a little to get another good look
at the first man he had ever made love
to. As he looked up he saw the waiter
in the mirror, who had sneaked in
unobserved, and as Juan looked closer
to the motion of the waiter's hand he
watched him cum across the bathroom
floor next to them. Juan didn't care.
He leaned in for another kiss, his dick
still inside Tomm, and starved for
affection as he had been he held him
for a few minutes longer regretting the
fact that he would have to clean up and
finish dinner as though none of it had
taken place. Tomm held him close and
whispered "Tomorrow."

Chapter Three

In the Future

About Harvey

Harvey's complexion had been repaired the first time he stepped into one of the dry showers here in White City. Dry showers had been one of the inventions His grandfather had created. They worked for anyone, but they had an extra benefit for those of the bloodline. All of his grandfather's inventions in some way gave extra benefit to the Tomm family. The dry shower fixed external tissue damage as well as removing dirt and dead, dry, flaked skin. So Harvey had perfect, unblemished skin now. His mother still enjoyed her normal skin. She didn't need any help anyway.

Harvey never had fully understood the bonuses that were included with the inventions. As far as he could tell his grandfather had been obsessed with equality. Extras for family only didn't seem to promote equality.

Harvey was bored. He didn't need to work and sometimes he just didn't know what to do with himself.

He stepped into the living room where his mother was napping on the sofa. He stood for a moment looking his mother over. She had changed since they had moved. The famous Tomm City food had transformed her from the overweight woman he knew as mom into a fine looking pepper haired seductress. Her clothing was no longer the rags of the swamps, but instead was the sheer synthetics of Tomm City, which besides being totally disposable left little to the imagination.

As beautiful as she was, Harvey felt no stirring in his flaccid penis. Women held no sway over him. Only men had graced his bed, and no one had graced it for quite a long time.

Harvey turned and stepped back out onto the patio.

Most inhabitants of Tomm City wore no clothing. His mother was one of the few who insisted. Harvey would have worn cloths himself but only one type of fabric could be made here and kept. The cleaners quickly destroyed any non-living organic materials, even while you were wearing them.

Harvey had tried to keep his leather jacket and boots for a while. He'd kept them locked up unless he was wearing

them. He had purchased them years ago
for bar hopping when he had lived up
north in Chicago. Jeans, T-Shirt, Belt,
Boots, Motorcycle Chaps and Jacket had
been kept safely for a month until he
had worn them out on the town as
novelties, gotten very drunk one
evening and passed out. When he awoke
in the morning they were gone. The
cleaners had taken them right from his
body. It kind of gave him the heebie-
jeebies when he thought about it too
much. That's what cleaners did.

Cleaners looked a lot like watchers.
They were the same shape anyway, like
crabs, but much smaller. It was their
chore to get under cracks in the doors
or through small openings. They found
dead organic matter and broke it down
until it was nothing more than dust
then carried it away. That at least was
how they worked everywhere else in the
world, which left rayon, polyester and
other synthetics alone. Within White
City they worked a little different.

Every nonliving thing within White
City was made of salt. Even if a lump
of granite were brought into White City
the cleaners would turn it to salt
within an hour if it wasn't placed
within a protective salt jar.

Which brings us to what made the
Tommy family so wealthy. It was
Harvey's Grand Daddy who had discovered

the alchemical formula that took common
salt and crystallized it to a solid
state that didn't dissolve, couldn't be
broken, wouldn't melt, and was clear as
glass. It was the hardest substance
known to man. The stuff could cut
diamonds like diamonds could glass.

Everything in White City was made of
the stuff, even clothing if you wore
any. Harvey didn't because in order to
make clothing from hard salt that
didn't pinch and bite the fibers had to
be made so thin that they were
completely transparent. So why bother
dressing up. Most of the citizens here
felt the same as he. Especially since
keeping other types of clothing was
virtually impossible. Anyway clothing
was so rare here that it made people
stare.

The air blowing in off of the ocean
was getting a little cool now. Harvey
wasn't dissuaded from his perch though.
He was watching the clouds build. He
hoped for some lightning and thunder.

The tips of the waves were beginning
to turn white with the turbulence in
the water and soon the wind would stir
too strongly and Harvey would be forced
inside. Right now the cool wind only
tickled the hair on his balls. He was
enjoying the cool, and he stood
casually pinching one of his nipples
that had gotten hard from the cool air.

Harvey was a bit on the short and stocky side. He was very muscular although he worked out very little. It was a blessing since most of the men he knew would need hours in the gym daily if they wanted to bulk to his normal build.

He had inherited his fathers pale skin, but had his mother's dark, deep eyes and course hair. His full lips and furrowed brows left him looking a bit on the fierce side. He was looking himself over in the reflection on the glassy patio door. He didn't look bad standing outside rubbing his own tit and developing a bit of a rod.

He was a hairy variety. Not the kind of hair you generally want either. He was covered with it back and all. He had thought quite a few times of having some hair pattern laser surgery done, somehow he never did go through with it though. He felt he was supposed to look the way he did. Besides, he had found that with so many smooth bodies around he was sort of a novelty among men.

He was sometimes surprised how much the hair on his body turned people on. He liked that since he felt like he generally had no purpose and regularly filled that void with as much man on man sex as he could handle. The thought was giving him a startling hard on.

He brushed his had over the hair on
his chest and belly reaching for his
dick, and turned to face the incoming
storm again.

There was lightning striking out
there now and the clouds had reached
him. A bit of wet mist began to sift
down into the wind of the storm. The
occasional thunder made Harvey feel
small facing its big power.

With his dick in his hand he began
his own personal rebellion against that
power. Every stroke sang defiance
against it and it's unforgiving nature.

He was gaining momentum, his heavy
balls swinging with the rhythm,
occasionally bumping his inner thighs
as he really started enjoying the
thrill of jacking off. He was trying to
be a little quiet so he wouldn't wake
his mother who was napping just on the
other side of the window.

Lightning struck again and the rain
came. Sheets of warm tropical water
poured from the sky onto Harvey. He
turned his face up into it drinking in
bits of it as he breathed heavily,
rhythmically with his new growing need
to shoot his load off of the balcony
and into the sea. He was groaning now
as the water mixed with his body oils
and made his skin slick.

The extra bit of sensation that was
added where palm and fingers stroked

the soft skin of his stiff dick caused him to cum.

Harvey gritted his teeth as his wad shot out and away and he watched it as it vanished over the rail and into the rain and sea. He enjoyed the last few lingering strokes across his meat as the orgasm slowed to a comfortable and relaxed throbbing.

He let his grip relax from around his dick, and leaned against the rail, gripping it with both hands then looked up into the clouds and opened his mouth wide. He rarely got to enjoy the rain like this, and he ran his hands over his head feeling the water pour out of his hair and down his back.

Harvey laughed a little with his deep scratchy voice. Purpose would be nice, but until then sex would do. He loved sex.

Chapter Four

Past and Present

A Happy Marriage?

Juan was desperately seeking any
escape from his political wife and all
of her affiliates. It had been nearly
five months from the time she had bore
their son. She was still mad at him
about the naming of their boy. In a way
Juan had been so rigid about it just
because he knew it would make her
angry.

When she had gone into labor it had
been hard on her. Juan had sort of
hoped it would have killed her, but She
had lived, and for some months she had
been going over a list of the most
horrifyingly stale names for the baby
she could think of.

Juan felt that as a father it was
his right to name the first born boy of
the family, but he had long since tired
of fighting over it with Sue, so while
she was in recovery, and he was left to
speak with the doctor he voiced it and
held his ground. He had nearly come to
blows with the Doctor over it. The man

kept on trying to consult his wife.
Juan had finaly stated that if lawyers
needed to be involved it could be
arranged. It was done while Sue slept;
the boy was named and baptized,
"Antonio Thomas".

Juan then carefully arranged to have
the press brought in so that his wife
could introduce her son to the people
she had bamboozled into thinking she
was honest.

When the baby was brought to her so
was the birth certificate and the
press. Even though she was clearly
unhappy it was never known why, with
the exception of Juan and the doctor.
With the camera pointed at her she
could only smile and play along lest
she embarrass herself in front of her
people, however, when no one was around
to see her but Juan she threw a fit the
likes of which Juan had never before
seen.

"We talked this over! We agreed on
Fredrick Sebastian!
How could you do this to me!" She had
screeched at in the loudest voice she
could muster.

Juan ignored her entirely. Their
marriage had been over even before the
baby had been conceived. As happened
with most of their arguments he fell
into his fantasies about a life with
Tomm. Juan's wife believed they were

just friends, but they'd been involved
in a torrid affair since the day they'd
met at the restaurant. Just thinking
about it was arousing Juan, even
through the bitching and screaming that
surprisingly hadn't woken the baby.

Huffing she realized her screaming
was having no effect and grabbed a book
from the table and as quickly as she
could struck Juan across the face with
it.

Startled Juan grabbed her wrists.

"I think you have forgotten that you
are a woman." Juan said in a deadly,
quiet voice." Then he grinned realizing
that he was still aroused from his
fantasy. "I think I had better remind
you about what it means."

Juan slapped her hard enjoying the
fear in her eyes.

"Are you glad you have finally
gotten a response? You've been goading
me on for years now, challenging me."

The sudden fear in her eyes pleased
him. He struck her again. This time she
cried.

"What should a wife do for her
husband?" Juan whispered into one of
her ears as she began to struggle. "You
should serve me. When I call for you I
want you ready to do as you're told."

"I…" She stammered.

"Oh your sorry now? Maybe you should
have thought about that before you

started saying anything you could think
of to piss me off!" Juan's voice grew
stronger.

Her eyes grew wider. "Maybe you
should have thought before you hit me
with your book there and gave me excuse
to put an end to your very bad
behavior!"

"A wife isn't just a servant!" She
retorted beginning to find herself
again. Juan wanted no argument. He
struck her again. The swollen red spot
on her face pleased him in some dark
instinctual way. He realized that he
had quite a rod in his slacks.

"Your no wife!" He spat. "A wife
would have more respect for her man
than you."
He slapped her again and spun her
around so she was looking away from him
and he threw her on the floor.

"You're a bitch is all. Just a lousy
little woman I married so I could
impress my parents."

It was true in every way Juan
realized. He had never married her for
love. She was a trophy, and good
breeding stock.

"You my dear are just a hole to
stick."

He fumbled with his zipper as he
pressed himself down on her, and he
quickly tore her blouse from her back.
She tried to get away, but he grabbed

her hair and forced her back to the
floor.

"What are you doing?" She cried
suddenly realizing how much stronger
Juan was than her. She was scared and
hurt.

"I'm getting even!" Juan raised his
voice for a moment as he tore her
skirts away. "For all of the times you
have treated my like shit in public.
I'm going to make you hurt just as bad
as you hurt me over the years we have
been married. I'm going to fuck you as
hard as I can, and while I'm doing it
I'm going to pretend you're someone I'm
attracted to. I'm going to pretend you
are worth something instead of the
worthless, bitching, conniving, cow I
married. I'm going to pretend you're a
whore, because that would be better
than what you are."

Juan quickly twisted one of her arms
behind her back so she couldn't get
away and without taking a moment to wet
her he shoved the entire length of his
dick deep into her from behind.

She screamed from the pain.

He quickly thrust again and again
the whole time thinking about Tomm's
sweet ass, Tomm's beautiful hard body,
and Tomm's hard dick. It was amazingly
easy to fuck her through her screams,
and even easier to enjoy it than he had
ever remembered. He came quickly, and

immediately pulled free. He zipped up and threw some of the rags he had made of her clothing at her as she lay weeping on the floor.

"Get dressed you slut! I think it's time we kept separate rooms. That was the worst fuck I've ever had."

Juan knew the words stung and startled her because he had never even really raised his voice at her before that night. He meant it too. He didn't want her anymore.

"Go to your bed and think about the horrible mess you've made of your marriage you sick political hypocrite." With that Juan walked from the room to go get a drink.

Juan slept fitfully in a perpetual state between the pleasure of what he'd done, coupled with intense guilt and a twisted sense of justification. It was somewhere in the fits of his troubled sleeping that he got an idea. He hated what life had turned him into. Yet he could clearly see what he wanted to become. He saw a strong man of principle. He realized that he had played the role his entire life but just playing the part isn't enough to make you what you want to be. Within his soul searching he saw something better. Someone stronger than he, someone weathered from the experiences of living but who had not grown course, but instead polished from hardships.

Juan awoke to the sound of his new baby crying with the idea he'd had on the edge of vision, yet hidden from conscious grasp.

"Sue!" he hollered through the house from his study. "The baby needs to be fed." There was no response.

Juan stirred himself from the couch where he had slept and went to the baby's room. He picked up Anthony and went in search of his wife. He found the bedroom in shambles.

Sue had packed her bags in a hurry and left. She had, however taken the time to write a very understandably bitter and hateful note.

"Keep your name for that screaming brat. I never wanted children with you. I wish I had never spawned the thing. I hope I never see you, your child or your stupid inventions ever again."

Juan was a bit startled. He hadn't thought she would leave so quickly. He'd figured she would try to maintain the family picture for her political agenda's. Still the fact he had underestimated her wasn't at the forefront of his thoughts. The baby needed to be fed. He went to the kitchen, but found that there wasn't any milk. Juan was stumped. He thought about where he could go to feed his boy while the tiny thing cried. The stores were all closed, and the only place Juan could think of was Tomm's so he wrapped Anthony in a blanket, threw on a coat and went out to brave the night streets. He wondered how Tomm would react to the situation.

The restaurant was locked up tight, and Tomm lived upstairs. The only access being through the restaurant behind the kitchen. Juan threw a few stones at the upstairs window that he imagined was Tomm's until he saw a light come on.

Anthony was getting pretty angry about his hunger and was crying quite loudly. When the window opened Juan could see that Tomm was angry about being woken until he saw who it was, but he was still startled.

"I'll be down in a moment." He hollered from the window.

In a moment Juan saw a light in the kitchen, then he heard the lock turning. Juan looked out the door into the cool night air. When he heard the baby crying he looked startled once again and motioned them inside.

"I'm sorry to disturb your sleep Tomm. I have nothing in my house to feed my boy. Do you have any milk?"

"Where's your wife?"

"I'm not sure, and I hope she doesn't come back."

Tomm frowned. "Left you did she?"

"We had a bit of a fight."

Juan followed Tomm into the kitchen where Tomm filled a pot with water and began to heat it then went to the cupboard and pulled out a very old baby bottle that he filled with milk from the cooler.

"The bottle was used to feed me once. I've been wondering for a while why I kept it." Tomm smiled as he set the bottle full of milk into the now steaming pot to warm the milk.

Juan was bouncing the baby to keep him quiet.

"You look God Damn sexy holding a baby." Tomm remarked.

Juan was suddenly very glad he had come here. Tomm had a way of taking the stress away. Juan leaned into the burly man for a quick kiss.

Tomm reciprocated then pulled away before the baby could get a hand full of his chest hair.

The bottle was warm now and Tomm fetched it and handed it to Juan. The baby was famished and took the old nipple without hesitation. Soon he was making comfortable sucking noises. Juan smiled down at his boy.

"At least my marriage wasn't a total failure." He said halfway to himself.

"I have a fine looking boy." Tomm
stepped closer and placed a hand over
the baby's head. The peach fuzz hair
was soft and warm.

"Why don't you stay here tonight?"

"I was hoping you might offer. It's
not just the chance to sleep with you
either. I don't want to go home, it's
not comfortable. I guess it never was."

The baby was asleep soon and after
arranging a few pillows on a small sofa
and pulling it close to the bed Tomm
and Juan undressed and amongst other
things fell asleep in each other's
arms.

Juan stayed home amongst the finger
pointing and political whisperings for
several months before he realized that
the note Sue had left him had been
honest. She wasn't coming home. The
police never found her. The missing
person scenario wasn't worth much
effort after the note. They had given
up locating her in a hurry. She didn't
want to be found. Juan wasn't too
worried about it. The only ones who
were concerned were her family. Still a
few months later Juan sold the house
and everything in it and moved into the
flat with Tomm above the restaurant
where they had first met.

He became quite a popular story
among the upper class of the city. It

was scandal. His wife had obviously
left him because he was homosexual.
They never would grasp the truth. She
had left for her own reasons. She
should have never been there in the
first place. She had never wanted to be
married. It was a sham from the start.

Juan wasn't interested in the petty
New York gossip though. He was in love,
really in love for the first time in
his life. The best part was that Tomm
reciprocated. With the money from the
house Juan had sold there was enough
money to get him started with his
inventions, and with Tomm cooking and
running his restaurant and the love
they shared all there needs and desires
were met.

Then the dreams began.

When it first happened Juan had
awoken abruptly from a sound sleep. The
sweat on his brows was obvious. He
looked over to see Tomm looking at him,
concerned.

"I was about to wake you. Should I
have?"

"It was terrible and frightening,
but I can't remember a thing about it."

"A dream?" Tomm asked.

"A dream." Juan responded.

"John? I haven't asked you about
your inventions in some time. Are you
doing well?" Juan had Americanized his
name to John Anthony vs. Juan Antonio a

few months ago. Tomm had always known
him as John. He had simply gone with it
when his marriage had ended. It seemed
an appropriate coarse of action since
his previous life was over and he was
starting fresh.

John frowned at the question put to
him.

"I still haven't come up with
anything good. I feel like a failure."

"Maybe that's why you have been
having these nightmare's."

John was a little startled. "You
mean I have been doing this a lot?"
John asked.

"All month, but I never dared wake
you."

John shuddered. He'd lied when he
said he couldn't remember a thing. He
could. There was a man in the shadows
talking to him. He could see the man's
silhouette but nothing discerning. It
was the voice that frightened him. It
was familiar, but he could never put a
finger on it. The presence that came
from the man in the dream was
intoxicating. He felt washed away by
it. Lost in a sea of thoughts when the
man spoke. John was scared of what the
man in his dream wanted from him.

"Next time wake me up." John said.

Tomm nodded.

"It's not my work that's causing
them. I don't know what it is."

It was little Antonio Thomas who spawned John's biggest invention. The years had passed quickly and Anthony was at an age where he was tearing apart his clothing faster than he could grow out of it. The child wasn't hyper active, just into some very rough activities. Anthony wrestled constantly with anyone willing. It left his jeans torn at the knees, and his shirts stained and tattered.

John had gone through all types of fabric but had yet to find one that wouldn't have holes in it by the day after he bought it. John decided to make a new fabric. He started with the idea of old chain mail, but the thought of putting a four year old in chain clothing was ridiculous. It would have to be lighter. Then John thought on making a fine chain mesh with something as hard as steel but much lighter. He began experimenting.

Nothing worked. John had worked himself into a migraine and so he lay down to nap. Through the exploding pain in his head he saw it.

He wasn't asleep yet, but he was having the dream. Fear gripped him as he realized he couldn't wake up to save himself. The man approached him staying just far enough away for John to see no visible facial features. John wanted to

run away. When the man spoke his voice
carried far to loudly to be natural for
the man didn't scream. John cringed
into himself but couldn't look away.

"*Finally I have a worthy servant
here on this forsaken planet. The thing
you want to create is yours if you
promise to serve me when the time
comes.*" The voice rumbled inside of
him.

"What thing?" Johns voice sounded
weak although he was screaming.

"*Indestructible armor.*" John thought
about the cloth he was trying to make.

"How will I have to serve you?" John
asked almost in a whisper.

The figure stepped closer and for
the first time he saw the face of his
greatest fear. "*I promise I wont ask
for more than you are willing to give.*"
Johns own voice spoke to him. "*Will you
serve me?*" His own face questioned. The
man in his dreams had been himself.

"Yes." He responded. As soon as the
words were spoken he was awoke to a
sharp slap on the face and Tomm was
looking down at him.

"Are you alright?" Tomm asked.

"Fine." John said. "And I have a
great idea." Suddenly John was terribly
aroused. "You just slapped me, can I
have a kiss too?"

"I'll kiss you for stud service."
Tomm's worried expression being

replaced by his own arousal. Tomm
leaned in and planted a hard kiss on
John.

John pulled on his long, hard,
throbbing cock in one quick motion
while the kiss was laid.

Tomm pulled away long enough to see
what had just happened. He grinned for
a moment at the thick vein covered
stick and then slowly placed his lips
over the huge shiny head.

John groaned. It had been a while
since they had taken interest in each
other like this and it was long over
do. John shivered as Tomm continued his
way down the length of the monster
between his legs. John felt the back of
Tomms throat relax against the pressure
of that rod as Tomm went all the way
down until John's balls ware pressed
soundly against his stubbly chin.

Tomm was a master at blowjobs, and
in no time was bobbing up and down on
John's dick in smooth motions. John was
amazed at how quickly Tomm could bring
him to the edge of an orgasm. Tomm must
have recognized the power of the moment
and stopped moving long enough to keep
the juice from spilling out. Instead he
stopped sucking and went in for another
kiss.

John noticed that during the sexual
exchange Tomm had kicked off his
boxers. John followed suit kicking off

his. Before long they were both
undressed.

Tomm relished the feel of his own
huge dick rubbing the furry hair above
John's dick. He loved the feel of their
dicks sliding up against one another
but as much as he enjoyed that he
wanted something else. He went down on
John once more and after getting John's
cock good and wet he positioned himself
and slowly lowered himself down onto
the stiff wet dick. Tomm groaned as
Johns shaft slid inside of him. He
leaned forward slightly so that he
could ride it the way he wanted it.

John closed his eyes as he let his
hands fall into place on Tomm's hips
and began to shiver as his dick was
slid rhythmically into and out of that
velvet, silky cock pocket. He imagined
in his head what it must look like back
there. He imagined his own long dick
slipping smoothly in and out of that
pinkish pucker. He opened his eyes to
look at the hard hairy chest of his
life long love, enjoying the feel of
Tomm's big pecker sliding and bouncing
around on his belly. He loved the smell
of their lovemaking and he was thinking
of no one but Tomm as he let himself
climax and released every bit of cum
that his nuts could muster together
into Tomm's silky soft insides.

Tomm groaned with the throbbing and lay down across John's chest, and for hours they just laid there with John's dick still inside of Tomm, holding each other.

Chapter Five

In the Future

God and Goddess

The breeze that had been blowing threatened to become a gale force wind now and the rain was getting cold. Besides, Jarren had contacted Harvey earlier in the week. Sometimes Harvey avoided the man in trade for some peace and quiet but he had been peaceful for too long this time around. A little bit of time out on the town would do him well.

Jarren was a half brother, one of many half brothers who Harvey hadn't even known he'd had until he'd moved to White City. There were so many half siblings here that Harvey still hadn't met. He doubted he would ever meet them all and he really didn't wish to. There were so many that the fact that they were family at all seemed like a joke.

Harvey had met Jarren in one of the local bars.

Jarren was a white boy while Harvey was a little on the dark side. They had both laughed a lot about the way they

had come to riches here the night they
met, and later they had gone to
Jarren's new flat and once there had
wild, intense sex.

It had been obvious to Harvey from
the get go that Jarren wouldn't be much
more than a one nightstand. Still he
had made very few friends in White City
and it was nice to have someone around
who cared.

Jarren was on the obsessive side
though and continued pressing Harvey
for more.

Harvey turned and left the patio
overlook. The storm would get dangerous
soon. He looked his sleeping mother
over once more and left to meet Jarren.

The bar where Jarren and Harvey had
decided to meet was the same one where
they had met the first time.

Harvey ordered a shot then took a
seat at his favorite table. It was nice
here. Everything was plush so you
couldn't stick if you sat too long. A
good thing since virtually everyone in
White City went naked.

Jarren took a seat across from
Harvey.

Harvey noticed that Jarren was a
little turned on. Jarren definitely had
it over Harvey in the dick size area.
Harvey was just a standard, even
average size man in that department.

Jarren's dick wasn't any longer than Harvey's, but it was a bit thicker.

"You like what you see there?" Jarren asked.

Harvey looked away realizing he had looked for too long and notice had been taken.

"It's okay, relax Harvey. We're just out for a drink."

"I know." Harvey explained, "but something has me on edge. I just can't place a finger on it."

"Exactly." Jarren said.

Harvey looked at the man expectantly thinking that someone else might feel it too.

"That's why I wanted to get you out of your house. So you can relax a little."

Harvey groaned. It was too much to hope that Jarren of all people would really understand. He probably just thought Harvey was paranoid.

"Bartend? How bout a shot of the heat for myself and a hit of green haze for the man." Jarren ordered.

"Jarren that shit costs a lot of dough!" Harvey scolded. "We might be well off, but it's on an allowance."

"Don't worry about it. I've been saving a little and it's on me tonight." Jarren retorted. "Besides, green haze is your favorite, right?"

"You have me there."

The shot of heat and the hit of
green haze were set on the table.
Harvey eyed his hit.

"You're right Jarren. I do need to
relax."

Harvey picked up the shot glass that
contained his drug of choice and
swirled it around in its container a
little. He eyed the green liquid
knowing what would become of the week
to come once he drank it. He would
spend twenty minutes or so with a
fairly normal thought process, then a
greenish cast would settle over
everything. He wouldn't be emotional.
He would be horny, and the world would
be like his favorite old black and
white subtitled film. He, of course
would be the star.

"Bottoms up." Jarren said as he
raised his glass to Harvey's.

"Get it in ya." Harvey said as they
clinked glasses and then downed their
drinks.

Harvey didn't understand Jarren's
love of the drink heat. It tasted like
water, made you feel uncomfortably warm
like you were lit on fire after being
soaked in kerosene before it began to
consume your flesh, and it made you
drunk fast, too fast for Harvey.

"Harvey?" Jarren asked.

"Yes?" Harvey responded.

"Before you get too drunk I better
ask. I had planned to go to an alley
party tonight. You interested?"

"Yeah, that'd be alright. When you
wanna go?"

"I don't know. An hour or so."
Jarren arranged.

When the haze hit the only color
other than black and white was green.
Harvey felt smooth and sexy. He
realized that he probably wouldn't
remember most of the week but during
the excursion it would all be good fun.

They arrived at the ally where the
party had been planned.

Harvey smiled. One of the men was
the guy Harvey bought his Sunday paper
from on the corner. Harvey had always
wondered what the man looked like with
a hard on. The man was hairy and Harvey
liked that.

The night progressed into an orgy of
sex. Men did men. Men did women. There
was everything. In Harvey's hazed
condition he just let it all happen. He
loved it.

After a while time blended so that
he didn't even know how long he had
been there. He'd had sex with at least
thirty men, one after another, their
wet cum had gotten all muddled together
inside him and every new penetration
promised a little more. The love of men

was wet and coated the insides of his thighs.

He was so exhausted he knew he wouldn't make it home that night. So he just laid down on the floor of the alley, men fucking all around him, and fell asleep inside his own personal black and white subtitled porn movie.

Harvey rubbed the black satin between his thumb and forefinger. It felt nice. The air in the house smelled different, more like his old home in New Orleans. He just laid there in bed listening to the sound of the man behind him breathing.

Harvey was quite disoriented. He had done a very expensive drug. He wasn't in White City anymore, and this concerned him. He rolled over to get a look at his bed companion.

The man next to him was astonishingly good looking. Perfect, some people might say. Harvey couldn't see signs of a blemish ever having happened in the man's life reflected in the man's tight and unwrinkled skin. His muscles were well shaped, as though he had been lifting weights his entire adult life.

Harvey found himself breathing a little more quickly now than when he had first awakened. Not from fear or confusion but from a form of hunger that was taking him.

The only thing that denoted age on the man was the color of his hair. It was all snow and silver, yet it was fine and soft looking, like bunny fur.

What Harvey could see of the man's chest was also covered with the downy white hair. Harvey wondered how he had stumbled across this handsome creature. The last thing he remembered was the alley where he had passed out.

The man stirred.

Harvey's penis stiffened.

The man awoke.

"I see you're feeling a bit better now." The man said to Harvey, sitting up in bed.

Harvey was astonished at how beautiful the man's lower torso fit into the rest of him. Now he could see most of the man's body. The blanket still lay over the man's groin leaving a lot for Harvey to imagine. Harvey's eyes involuntarily followed the line of fur down the man's belly toward an unseen end.

"Where am I?" Harvey asked sleepily and a bit dreamily. Harvey was glad that the green haze didn't leave a hang over, just light dizzy euphoria.

"Not far from your home. I live on the coast. White City is just on the horizon."

The man leaned in for a kiss. Harvey groaned and let the man fall over him.

Chest to chest now, Harvey savored the feel of the man's hair against him. It was soft like bunny fur.

The man's mustache tickled Harvey's upper lip and the way his tongue mingled with Harvey's was heaven.

Harvey let his hands slide down the man's back toward his buttocks, which were also covered in downy fur, then groaned and reached around to discover what was in front.

The man was frighteningly large. Harvey couldn't quite reach his fingertips completely around it, and it was the longest dick he had ever felt. He knew it was larger than he would be able to enjoy, but he craved it, wanted it inside him. He wanted to savor every inch.

The man seemed to sense this and pressed in, motioning Harvey to turn over. Harvey acquiesced easily, rolling onto his stomach, enjoying the weight of the man on his back.

For a time the man teased Harvey, just rubbing that monster on Harvey's buttocks and between his legs.

Harvey groaned and when he thought he could stand no more the man pulled away for a second. Long enough to put some slick liquid onto his dick. When he returned it to the crack of Harvey's butt he slowly pressed and slid the entire length of it inside.

It should have hurt, being as large as it was, but all Harvey felt was enjoyment.

The man took it slow at first allowing Harvey to just enjoy the feel of every vein and contour of the big dick slowly slide in and out of him. After a few moments the pace quickened to a pounding.

Harvey was groaning loudly at the pleasure of it, the soft fur against him, the size of the dick inside him, the hot kisses on the back of his neck.

Harvey realized that the man had very large, low hanging, balls, large enough not only to slap against Harvey, but to swing right up between his legs and slap against his own plumb sized balls.

The hair on the man's nuts tickled every time they swung in and against Harvey's.

Harvey came with that thought fixed in his mind.

The man feeling the tightening and relaxing of Harvey's anus came in the same instant, dropping heavily onto Harvey.

Harvey fell asleep buried under the man, held tightly in a man's strong embrace.

Harvey awoke later in the day to find himself alone in a strange bed. He swung his legs out and over the side of the bed and looked around. He hadn't been in a state of mind to notice his surroundings completely. He just knew that he had started out in an alley with Jarren and had ended up on the mainland in an abandoned house. The only furniture appeared to be the bed he was in and the satin bedding.

Harvey stood up to look around. The place was large. Upstairs were six bedrooms, each with it's own bath. Downstairs were two kitchens, one for servant's quarters and one for the main house, a huge front entry with ballroom attached, a really nice dining room and a large library and study.

It was disturbing that there wasn't any sign that anyone had lived here in some time.

The house had been built in the classic style, all of organic material, no salt components. Even the windows were old glass. Harvey was surprised they weren't broken, and that there was no visible rot on the woodwork.

The only place Harvey had ever seen that was all organic before this was his mothers place on the swamps were he had been raised, and as far as he knew that was because they could never afford to upgrade.

Harvey thought back on his morning
and his mysterious lover. It had been
the best sex of his life and still
there seemed to be something missing,
something out of place in his mind.

Feeling disturbed, Harvey left the
place. It would only take a moment to
find a hover car to get him back to
White City. His mother would be worried
about him by now, and he was curious to
find out what had happened with Jarren.

Harvey's mother Trista rolled her
eyes back and forth under her sleeping
eyelids.

"You'll die!" She grumbled.

If Harvey had stayed for a second
longer he'd have heard her.

"Every last one of you miserable
creatures will be cleansed from my
surface. Your just another mistake, a
failure." Trista grumbled in her sleep.

Trista bolted to an upright
position. "Harvey?" she questioned the
air with wide, fear filled eyes. She
knew he needed help. He had no idea
what kind of danger he was in. It was
her fault in a way. Not for who she was
but for what she was. She had to tell
him, but he wasn't here.

Inside her it burned. She was a
witch woman, perhaps one of the last
truly strong ones. Her whole life she
had closed it within herself, but now

it was boiling for release. The power
was invading her sleep, whispering to
her. It warned her that she would die
here if she didn't run now. How could
she think to save Harvey if she
couldn't first save herself?

She jumped up to leave, hurrying for
the door. In her haste she ran straight
into the enemy. He grabbed her by the
shoulders as she tried to force her way
past him, his hands pinching into her
skin.

"No!" She exclaimed. "She mustn't
find me!" Why wasn't her glow bug
saving her from this man? He pushed her
back into the apartment turning her
around so he could put a hand over her
mouth as they moved.

The glow bug wasn't her only defense
though. If it wasn't effective she had
her witch power. It snapped inside her
like a whip instinctively looking for
the man in the room.

"None of that now." He said as he
threw her onto the sofa she had been
napping on moments before.

She looked up at her glow bug
expecting it to do something. It
flickered then turned to salt as it
fell to the floor. In that same moment
the fury of her witch power was frozen
over like a northern lake in a really
cold winter storm.

"She already has found you." The man said. "And you're not ready to face her yet."

Trista wanted to scream. She finally looked up and got a good look at the man. "You!" She yelped in surprise.

"You recognize me then?" He said as he began his spell. The sofa shook underneath her. She felt her muscles cramp in her arms as she involuntarily tightened her grip around the cushions. Her nose went numb first, then her pinky fingers and toes. She remembered mostly the smile on his face as she lost consciousness.

Gia faced off with Mars. She couldn't help but to be drawn to the man. His gray hair shone like a storm. She knew she would have to be cautious with this one. He was clever and immensely powerful. She had slept for far too long, and she knew that although she could master him she wasn't at her best.

Men had been her problem. She had left the planet in their charge and had slept for thousands of years. Men had forgotten their charge to care for her, and her surface had been bruised and cut. Her veins bled for ore. She despised the creatures she once had cradled.

Mars smiled at her. He had chosen a
very handsome vessel. It had been a
long time for her and her libido
groaned for him. He noticed her desire,
and she withdrew her gaze.

"I would like tea. Would you join
me?" She asked quizzically.

"Certainly." Mars responded, "May I
suggest someplace public." He added.

"Wonderful." She said but she had
hope for solitude with him. She
couldn't work a God Spell of the kind
she needed without close contact.

She jumped a little when Mars
snapped his fingers and flames consumed
them, but then she remembered his mode
of transport. There was no malice in
this little trick of his. She had only
slept for too long and was easily
startled. The flames flickered and she
found herself in a most lovely city
resting directly on the water's
surface. It was a more brilliant white
than any temple she had ever seen
before.

There were men everywhere moving
about. She groaned vengeance and raised
her hand to begin her cleanse of the
planet here but Mars was ready and
restrained her hand and magic. She was
startled by the power he had mastered
while she had slept. She stared at him
coldly.

"You can play later." He said. "We came here for tea and conversation."

She was once again drawn to him but was furious at herself and him. He had never had the power to directly intervene against her before. At least not while walking her planetary surface instead of his. "I can see the fury in you." He said. "You stand inside my temple here. This entire city is mine."

"We are having tea at your house then?" she queried. "You are showing off for me." She smiled a secret smile. Perhaps her plan would work rather well after all. He seemed interested in wooing her interest, in wowing her with his power.

"This is the third time you have interrupted my bath and face wash." She said. Referring to the cleansing of mankind from her planetary surface. "Why?" She asked as they walked into a pretty little coffee shop near where Harvey lived.

"I like men." Mars said. "They are quite resourceful. Since you are throwing them away. Can I have them?" He smiled at her.

Charming, she thought. He winked at her. "What are you going to do, transport them all to your surface? They would die."

"I will keep them here." He said.

She was quick with her slap. It was loud and drew the eyes of the humans in the café. "How dare you?" She spat! "What gall. Look at what these monsters have done to me." Then she smiled. "Choose another creature." She became suddenly aware that everyone in the place was staring way more at her than they should be. They were terribly frightened of her. Something was wrong. Mars had hidden something from her and she looked at him with a critical, appraising, and dangerous look. His smile was not charming this time but cunning and guile. "You keep dangerous secrets from me Mars." She said threateningly

"I don't want another creature." Mars said. "I want humans." The people in the café had begun cautiously filtering out all the while keeping an eye on her. She had never experienced such a reaction from one of her own creatures before.

"Be still." She said with her god power at them. Still they stepped away. *"Why don't they obey me?"* She thought. Instead they fled more quickly.

"You see that they become mine anyway." Mars said. Gia stood abruptly sending the light salt chair skittering across the floor behind her.

"You Son-Of-A-Bitch!" She said. "You have stolen my children."

"I have recycled your garbage." Mars said. He looked calm and unruffled.

"I will convene a council of Gods and have you recycled you thieving wart."

"Will you now?"

She darted for him with her fingernails and he easily moved from his chair and out of her way. He looked over his shoulder and saw Harvey outside the café looking straight at them and grinned his plan had worked perfectly. "It's time to go." He said smiling and snapped his fingers.

She tossed her hair to follow him leaving a shower of flower petals behind her as she chased the evil God. She would have his balls.

Outside there was a crowd of people staring into the café with fear in their eyes. Many of them had never seen an act of violence in their entire lives. They had only read of it in history. Seeing her slap him had raised fears that they themselves could be struck and they had fled.

Harvey who had seen the crowd on his way to lunch had not seen the violence, but having seen the crowd he had curiously stopped to look into the café. He was not afraid but stunned. He saw the man he had slept with and still dreamed of arguing with his mother. He

didn't even hesitate. He charged into
the diner only to find it empty when he
got inside, the floor covered with
flower petals and salt dust.

   "I must be going crazy." He thought.

Chapter Six

Past and Present

Invention

John had made it and he was the only
one who knew how it was done. He had
this filmy clear layer of cloth that he
found could be glued to the outside of
normal cloths making them
indestructible unless they were sprayed
with the counter formula which he
wouldn't reveal to anyone. This
invention would make him millions,
maybe more.

He thought of his son who would be
living in the lap of luxury for the
rest of his life. It made John happy.
His own life had been so torn with
doubts.

The only thing that really seemed to
bother Anthony was who and where his
mother was.

John couldn't tell him for a number
of painful reasons. He didn't want to
dig up the past. One of the reasons
being that Sue had resurfaced
unexpectedly and had continued her
political career and now stood a good

chance of becoming president. She wouldn't appreciate the scandal. John didn't want anything to do with her. He was sure she was incapable of human emotion. She would probably just try to use her son to obtain more votes.

"John?" Tomm popped his head in to see what was going on.

"You on lunch?" John asked.

"Yeah." Tomm replied.

"Good time to celebrate the greatest invention ever then." John said as he pulled Tomm to himself and cupped his buttocks warmly with his large hands and embraced him.

"Later love. I have the boy with me." John bit his lower lip.

"Hey dad." His son grinned as he stepped through the door. John gave Tomm one good kiss then let him go.

"How's my boy?" John asked as he stepped over and rustled Anthony's hair.

"Fine." Anthony grumbled as he squirmed to get away then made a disheveled attempt to straighten his hair back out. "Do you always have to do that?" Anthony said perturbed.

"You ready to be a rich kid?" John smiled.

"You did it dad?"

"You bet I did."

    The next few years were bliss. John
had developed a manufacturing plant and
there he had learned to make all sorts
of things with his formula. He made
panels for cars, windows, wove it into
fabrics. He had become quite wealthy,
and had also become quite well known,
he and Tomm. They were sort of like
role models for gay men out there. They
were out of the closet, domestic to the
point of raising a very healthy son
together, and they were rich.
    It couldn't last though. John was so
in love with Tomm, but Tomm had stopped
sleeping with him, and had in most ways
stopped showing interest. John barely
saw him, and when he did see him all
Tomm would talk about was how much he
missed the restaurant.
    "So buy a new one." John said one
night. "I want you to be happy."
    "You know I think I should." Tomm
said resoundingly.
    John was so busy with his own
business that he barely realized when
the day had come for Tomm to open back
up. He realized coldly that they hadn't
spoken in weeks, and that Tomm hadn't
bothered to invite him although others
were sure to be there.
    John had become increasingly
suspicious of Tomm lately. He was sure
that there was an affair going on
behind his back, but he couldn't bring

it up without proof. He just sat in his
chair and thought. That was when he
dozed off and had another idea.

*"Why don't you make a spy? Make it
one that is indestructible and small.
Make it alive after a fashion."*

John awoke with a start, and began
work on the first watcher, and like in
the dream when he was done it was self-
replicating.
Driven with the need to find out why he
was being left out of Tomm's life he
released it without thought of the
consequences.

As an after thought he made the
little creatures that would show what
the watchers saw. Little screens on
their backs. This one he kept inside a
little glass cage so he could watch it
and sent the other to spy on Tomm until
it was instructed otherwise.

Chapter Seven

In the Future

"Mommy"

Harvey was confused. Anyone would be were they found in his unusual circumstances. His mother had vanished without a trace, and now he had seen the man of his dreams twice. There was a definite mystery here. He fled back to his home and once again found a viewer so that he could track them down.

"State the location." The viewer said.

"The Mars Café." Harvey said.

"State the time you wish to view." The viewer said.

"Start from half hour ago to current." Harvey leaned back into a chair to watch. "Speed times five." He said.

The images sped forward. "Pause there." He said as his mother and the man he remembered from a few nights before suddenly appeared inside the café. He was startled.

"How did they enter?" he queried the viewer.

"Unknown." It replied.

Harvey continued to watch and soon discovered why people were running from the café.

Harvey was quite frightened at what he saw. A woman he had loved and trusted, his own mother, committing an act of violence. In that moment he discovered a layer of paranoia he had never thought could exist. He felt insecure and afraid. He thought about all the time he had spent sleeping under the same roof with her. She could have hurt him at any time. He shivered.

"Who is the man she hit?" he asked the viewer.

"John Tomm." Came the response. Startled Harvey stood up and started for the fridge for a drink. That's when the shakes hit him. He hit the ground and fainting before he even got close to the kitchen.

The swamps are full of beautiful and dangerous things, and some things that are ugly but harmless, and even some things that are just plain ugly. Just don't get too close.

"Why am I in the swamps?" Harvey thought.

Still he meandered his way around a very large snake that was quite beautiful but harmless. A mosquito bit him on the shoulder. He looked ahead into one of those places in the swamps that are like hidden treasures. Beautiful and un-approachable unless by boat or hovercraft neither of which Harvey had.

Gators swam thick here. Harvey wondered what they were eating to stay alive with so many of them gathered in one place.

A shack stood in the midst of this place. It was smothered in vines and surrounded by flowers that were only bright when the suns rays slanted through the huge cypress trees to touch them in lighted patches before the next cloud blew by. There was just enough ground mist to make the scene surreal and dream like.

Harvey saw his mother there. She walked into the shack looking quite angry, and the drape that covered the door fell closed. Harvey extended a hand to call out but was greeted by blackness.

When Harvey came to Jarren was standing over him with a smug grin and a glass of water. "This makes twice." He grinned as he handed Harvey the water.

Harvey sat himself up and drank. His throat was quite dry.

"Thanks." He said.

"No problem." Jarren said. "You might want to lay off of some of the heavy stuff Harvey. I might not be here to pick you up every time."

Harvey smiled. "I'm sorry you've had to clean me up so much lately. I'm not used to having my mother just disappear on me." Harvey said. "I need to find out what happened to her. I saw her today, what's really strange is that I saw grandfather."

"That can't be right." Jarren said looking a little perplexed. "He should have been dead a very long time ago."

"Have a look." Harvey said motioning to the screen. "The watchers see everything."

After a few moments of looking at exactly what Harvey had seen Jarren was done and was just as upset.

"What upsets me isn't so much Grandfather. He may have invented something that lengthens his life indefinitely for all we know." Jarren said. "It's the fact that your mother is immune to the effects of glow bugs, and that she doesn't have one anymore. I know I saw her hit grandfather. What if glow bugs are becoming ineffective. I mean they are really the only thing keeping the world from anarchy."

"I agree. That's why I need to find her."

"How much do you know about your mother Harvey?" Jarren asked after a moment of silent thought.

"I've lived with her my entire life." Harvey responded, a bit irritated that Jarren would ask such a dumb question. Of course, Jarren was blond, so Harvey thought he could cut him a little slack.

Jarren frowned at Harvey and one of his eyebrows twitched impatiently. "No, I mean details. Be honest. How much do you really know about her?" Jarren watched Harvey's face while the idea began to turn through Harvey's stressed head.

Harvey wished Jarren would stop looking at him like that. It was making him feel like he was the butt of a really big joke that everyone but himself got.

"I guess I really don't know anything about her life or the things she was up to while I wasn't around." Harvey admitted.

"Exactly!" Exclaimed Jarren.

Harvey still didn't get the point and it was obvious by the expression he was wearing that he needed a verbal explanation.

Jarren groaned in frustration. "And people tease me for being blond?"

"What are you getting at?" Harvey said exasperated. "Just spit it out."

"Find out stupid. What was your
mother up to before her disappearance?
There has to be some clue that will
lead you to her."

Harvey grumbled under his breath and
looked at the floor.

"Or maybe you need a break." Jarren
said as he slipped closer, leaning in
on Harvey. Harvey blushed and frowned.

"Maybe another time." He said, but
Jarren slipped him a little bottle.

Harvey looked at the little thing.
It was green. "You aren't going to
leave me in a alley with my own shit
dried to my legs this time are you?"
Harvey grumbled warning.

"I'll let you do the hokey pokey
this time." Jarren consoled him.

Harvey had to admit that he was
becoming aroused. He leaned back in his
chair so Jarren could bring him the
goods. He looked at Jarren's big dick
before he slid it into his mouth right
up to where Jarren's blonde bush was
mingling with Harvey's own prickly
facial hair.

Jarren groaned. Harvey was aware of
Jarren's premature ejaculation problem
and backed off quickly. Instead he
turned him around and bent him over.

Jarren's pink pucker looked
delicious and Harvey wasted no time
tongue fucking the thing. When Jarren
was again on the edge of climax Harvey

stopped and leaned back into the chair
again.

Jarren turned around and straddled
Harvey, carefully positioning Harvey's
now throbbing dick for full
penetration.

Harvey groaned and closed his eyes.
It was silk as Jarren's ass muscles
hugged every vein-covered inch of
Harvey's cock. Harvey took one deep
breath then unstopped the bottle and
downed his drug of choice before Jarren
leaned in for a kiss, then waited for
the world to fade into a green dream.
Harvey loved doing the Hokey Pokey.

Chapter Eight

Past and Present

Eavesdropping and Politics

John got what he wanted.

The watcher followed Tomm. John watched the other man making love to Tomm. He cried, not because he felt that Tomm had no right to make love with who ever he wanted, but because Tomm was not interested in him anymore. John wanted it to be the way it was when they had first fallen in love. He just wanted Tomm to want him again. He wished he hadn't even learned the truth of it all. He went to bed alone most of the time. Tonight he did the same, knowing that the man he loved more than anything in the world was lying in the arms of another man.

In the mean time the watchers got away from him. They began reproducing like wild fire. Inside the city where he lived they began looking over everyone. Whether they were making love in the privacy of their homes or whether it was a fistfight outside of a

local bar. The eyes of the watchers
were recording all.

What woke John the next morning was
the sound of the glass container he had
kept the counterpart of the watcher in
breaking. The viewer had multiplied in
the night until there were so many of
them that there was enough pressure to
break the glass. The anti privacy
plague had started.

Sue was quite perturbed. She had
spent the last ten years of her life
trying to erase what had happened to
her. She had never even finalized the
divorce. Then to have her estranged
husband show up as some awesome
inventor. She wanted the man to vanish
from existence. As for her son, she
shuddered to think that he had ever
been inside her, the child of a wife-
beating rapist. If the world really
knew the truth they would hardly have
given him such good media. Still his
formulae would be very valuable to her
military if she could secure it. She
was quite close to the Presidential
seat. Securing such a large
contribution to the military could very
likely buy her the elections and votes
she wanted. She would have support from
people who otherwise would turn on her
faster than she could imagine. Even
better was that she could finally get

even with Juan. She had the power to hurt him in many ways, and she relished it.

She picked up the phone to make some preparatory phone calls. A meeting would have to be arranged.

John had been deep in thought when the knock on the door to his study came.

"Dad? I know you don't like to be disturbed when you're in here but there are some men at the door."

The men at the door claimed to be secret service. They proclaimed that John would accompany them. He would be questioned as a possible threat to homeland security.

The car ride could have been comfortable had John wanted anything to do with the men he was with. The building they took him to was decadently furnished, and the room where he was seated was gaudy and soft.

"It's the nature of your invention that concerns us." One of the men was rambling on. "If the wrong persons were to get hold of it they would have a unstoppable military force which could leave us in a very compromised situation."

"Nobody knows the formulae but me." John said. "It has never been written down so that I could keep exactly that

from happening. I am aware that it
could be misused. That is exactly why
every piece of the stuff made has been
by me."

"Perhaps it could have been left in
your care before now, but your
government wants that formula."

"I won't give it to anyone."

"We can pay you for it."

"What guarantee do I have that my
government won't commit to exactly the
types of military atrocities that you
claim to want protection from." John
said. "The formulae will remain with
me"

"Perhaps we can change your mind."
The man prattled on "Bring her in."
John lifted his head in alarm.

"Juan?" Sue said as she came into
the room.

"Sue!" John jumped to his feet. His
surprise had gotten the best of him,
but he recovered quickly. "I go by John
now Sue."

"John then." Sue corrected herself.

John seated himself again and Sue
sat across from him.

"To what do I owe the pleasure?"
John said acidly.

"Just politics dear." Sue said as
she handed him some legal documents. "I
thought it was about time we made the
divorce final."

Suspicious John looked around the room then back at the divorce papers.

"Then there is the matter of custody of our son. Anthony wasn't it? It's been a while."

"You would use Anthony for political leverage? I must admit that I continually underestimate the depth to which you can sink Sue."

"Don't pretend you're so innocent John. Maybe the world would like to know why I ran away."

John's face turned red with fury.

"Just take the money John." Sue said. "All of this will go away, including me. You'll have full legal custody of Anthony and I'll walk away knowing we aren't connected anymore. It's what's best for us all."

And that is how the military got hold of the formula for indestructible armor.

John got home and knew he couldn't trust those people. He went in search of Tomm. He found him sitting in the back room with Anthony. They looked worried.

"What happened?" Tomm asked.

"My formula has been sold to the military."

Tomm jumped up. "Why would you do that? You know what they want it for. You've handed them the world on a silver platter."

"Blackmail! They threatened to take
Anthony." Anthony pulled his legs up
onto the couch and began to cry. "It's
okay son. I won't let them take you
away from us." John said as he moved to
give comfort.

"It's almost time." John said to
himself inside the dream.
"I'm not ready." John said.
"You made a deal with me. You can't
back out." Still maybe you should be
allowed to clean up your mess before I
return."
"Who are you?" John asked. "You look
and sound like me but you don't act
like me at all."
"Clean up your mess John."
"What mess?"
"The watchers for one. Then there is
my indestructible armor in the wrong
hands. How did that happened?"
"I love the boy. I couldn't just let
her have him."
"No I suppose you couldn't. I will
help you clean up this mess you've
made. Go south until I stop you. Don't
stop. They'll catch you. Even now they
are on you like hounds. Don't look
back."

"John?" Tomm nudged him. "You were
talking in your sleep again. You asked
me to wake you when it happened."

"I love you Tomm." John said.

John wasn't sure exactly how he had
made it to bed, and for many years he
wondered why he did it. It must have
been the dream, and then there was that
little bit of pent up jealousy.

"I know you've been seeing other
men." He announced. "I invented little
spies to catch you." Tomm rolled away
from him.

Argument ensued.

The argument ended with Tomm leaving
the house for a walk. He was angry and
needed some fresh air.

There was a haze in the air that
left a ring around the streetlights. It
was cold. Tomm didn't think anything of
the limousine turning the corner toward
him so he didn't expect it to stop.

Before he could cry for help the
window rolled down and a gun was
pointed at him. He was shot, but not a
bullet, a tranquilizer.

He stared disbelieving at the red
end of the dart sticking out of his
shoulder before the world turned black.

Chapter Nine

In the Future

A God's Seduction

Trista awoke in the humid air of a
swamp that looked strikingly familiar.
She knew this place. She had grown up
here, but it had never looked like
this. She knew she had been taken, but
she wondered why she had just been
taken here. She was alone too. Why was
she alone?

Trista climbed out of her old
hammock and began to wander around the
place. It should be in ruins, but
instead it appeared that the plants
around it had lifted it up and tied it
all together. The flowers were
spectacular, and the perfume in the air
could only make her smile.

The hut she had grown up in was on a
low island in the swamps. Outside, it
was raised off of the ground with log
stilts for high water. There were times
when the water would nearly enter the
hut. Right now the water was quite low
though, and she felt comfortable just
wandering. She remembered her mother

raising her out here, all alone. Her
mother had been a witch woman, and
preferred solitude. The swamps were
safe for a witch. They were not always
safe for others. Gator filled waters
surrounded her mother's little island
and then there were other things too,
but only a witch would know them.

"Hello Trista." The man's voice
purred behind her.

She jumped and again reached for her
power. It remained frozen over. She was
helpless. She turned around but she
already knew who it was. It was the man
who had kidnapped her, but how could he
know of this place?

"Anthony." She said as she turned
around to face him. "You've gone all
gray."

"Ha." The man laughed. "My son did
look rather like me didn't he?" John
said.

Trista squinted through the eerie
light of the swamp for a clearer look.

"John? But why?"

"Shh." John put his finger to his
lips. "She sleeps. I don't want to wake
her. It took a lot of strength for her
to confront my master. He seems to
think you will help us. I think it is a
mistake to trust a woman."

"Help you with what?" Trista said
irritably. She didn't like that last

comment. Besides shouldn't this guy be dead?

"Help us hide Harvey." He said.

Trista's eyes got suddenly wide. "From who?"

"From your mistress. From the one you serve weather you are conscious of it or not. She doesn't take servants like my master who leaves me free to live on my own for the most part. When she takes a servant she takes full power over them. The only reason you are awake and she is now asleep is because we, Mars and myself, wiped her out with a mere conversation. She almost took us out though."

"Tell me more." Trista commanded.

"Yes, but there isn't much time and time is of the essence. You serve the earth. She is the mother of all that exists upon the surface of this world. She calls herself Gia, but has taken many women as her servants, Aphrodite, Venus are just a few. None could keep secrets from her. We think you are strong enough. Usually she doesn't choose a witch as strong as you, but there were limited women to choose from. She wouldn't want a weak witch either. It would leave her at a disadvantage."

"So you are the one who kidnapped me?"

"Yes, but only to keep Harvey from her. He is unique. We took you far from him in an effort to hide him from her before she took you. We were almost too late."

"How can I trust you?" Trista asked suspiciously. "Without my power I can't tell if you lie."

"I apologize." John said. "It was a necessary precaution."

John let go of his spell on her. She shivered as the biting chill ebbed away and the warmth of her power filled her again. "Touch me then with your witch power and know that I tell the truth."

Trista reached out and touched his brow and felt his sincerity wash over her. She was startled slightly, but after all Harvey was his grandson.

"What shall I do then?" Trista asked.

"Here." John said as he handed her the potion he had made. "You must drink this." Trista looked at it nervously. "It won't hurt you. It will allow you to watch but not take part in the actions she does with your body, and it will allow you to take control when she is resting like now. I will return to teach you the nature of your own power when she is asleep although it is a great risk to me."

"Why would you put yourself in such danger?"

"Because when she discovers that you are holding secrets from her she will try to dispose of you so that she can find a new vessel. I will teach you how to protect yourself from such things so that she cannot leave you. She is trapped in you. Just like you are trapped by her. She just doesn't know it yet. My relationship with Mars is much the same way but he has known it was so for millennia. That is why he seeks out servant's he can trust."

"How long do I have to prepare myself?" She asked.

"We don't know, but we think she will seek more strength first. I am sorry that you will have to watch. She will take many men and from them she will obtain great strength. Then she will grow curious about you and she will press her mind onto you. You have at least one lunar cycle. She believes herself week from long rest, but it is only because I defeated her. She is stronger than Mars has ever been though. The only reason she didn't succeed is because I am a man who loves other men. Still I was nearly drawn into her spell."

Trista looked at the potion again. "For Harvey." She said as she downed the draught. When she looked back up John was gone.

Harvey sank into his bed with the hazy green light surrounding him. Green could last for some time depending on the mix, weeks even. In a world where violence wasn't a concern people could relax and fall into mind altered states without worrying about the dark side of their nature committing atrocities while they were under the influence of such chemicals. Jarren had gone home some time ago and had left Harvey resting on the sofa. After a while Harvey had gotten up and made a drink then slipped through the dry shower and gone to his room for a nap. The clear but surprisingly warm and soft bedding nestled around him.

It had taken much for him too get used to the quiet of White City. It would be hard to leave now, and Harvey would leave soon to find his mother. He was quite worried about her. He rolled over to find he wasn't alone.

"Sleep well Harvey. John said as he leaned in and kissed Harvey heavily on the lips. You don't know your value yet. I need you more than you can know."

Harvey was stirred to erection instantly upon seeing his grandfather. The man was perfect, and the man was dressed. The suit coat hung on the man's shoulders in just such a way, and the pants curved around his goods in

just such a way. It sent Harvey's
imagination into overtime as he
imagined what was hidden underneath,
out of sight. Harvey leaned into the
man and ran his hand down the cotton
covering his chest then down the rough
denim of his jeans. The erection there
was huge and Harvey wanted it, needed
it inside of him. He fumbled with the
button and zipper but was unaccustomed
to such things and in his drugged
stupor was unable to unfasten anything.
John did it for him. His dick was huge
compared to Harvey's. Harvey looked it
over trying to remember how it had
looked the last time.

*"Why does the man only show up when
I'm on green?"* Harvey thought.

It was definitely perfect. It jutted
straight out from the man. There were
no bends to the left or right like most
of the others Harvey had seen and the
thick veins ran symmetrically from the
top down the sides. The foreskin was
there, but it wasn't overly long and it
hugged the swollen, throbbing head
tenderly. Harvey went for it, mouth
open but stopped. John was taking off
his jacket. Harvey fell back into the
bed and watched the man undress. He
watched as the man undid the buttons of
his cotton shirt with his big, strong
hands. The amount of hair on the man's
broad chest made him look furry more

than hairy. It wasn't gray, but silver
and shiny. The green seemed to
evaporate from Harvey's mind when he
looked directly at John. Harvey knew
the man should look old, but there
wasn't a wrinkle, line, or blemish. His
smooth, olive skin was bumped only with
thick veins that pressed out against
the taught skin where the thick muscles
of a hard, working man moved. Harvey
thought he might cum just from looking
at the chest and forearms. He rubbed
his own dick a little, but not too
much. He wanted to enjoy this. He
wanted to remember this, although he
doubted he would with the amount of
green he had drunk.

Harvey began tugging lightly on the
tangled hair of his balls while John
took off his trousers. His fingers
tickled lightly as they tried
ineffectively to pull the kinked hair
straight. It was not like John's silver
hair that also thickly covered his
balls legs and ass. John's hair was un-
kinked and looked so soft. Harvey
groaned as John finally came into the
bed and lay down against him. He had
been right. Having the man next to him
felt like humping a soft fur coat. The
man's wet kiss had him on the edge.
Harvey shivered all the way though.

John went down, pressing Harvey's
legs up against his own belly and with

strong swipes of his tongue rimmed circles around Harvey's hole.

Harvey gripped as much of the blankets into his hands as he could and clenched his teeth. The man knew what he was doing. Harvey wondered why he hadn't came. The end of his dick was on fire with pleasure.

John mounted him swiftly and fiercely. The speed in which that huge cock dropped into Harvey's ass should have hurt horribly, but it didn't.

Harvey groaned as it filled him up, in more ways than one. He could feel the skin inside him, but he also felt a connection with this man that he had never felt before. He felt like he was part of everything that existed when the man touched him. He felt the pulse of the twirling sun, hot inside him with every thrust of thick, moist dick. He cried out when John came because he could feel distinctly every throbbing burst of fluid as it sank into him. His body wanted it. He felt like he was absorbing it as it flooded him. He doubted that any of it would drip out when John pulled out. John didn't pull out though. Instead he fell heavily on top of Harvey, which is where he stayed.

They both fell asleep.

The next morning Harvey woke up alone. There was no trace of John.

Harvey wondered if he had been
dreaming.

It would be years before he would
see the man again …

Harvey had been expecting more smoke
in the bar but he knew that later there
would be plenty of smoke. Why he even
came in was beyond him but then it was
one of his old hangs. He didn't
remember names, but then it was nice to
be a stranger again, and faces still
were familiar enough for him to know
whom he had met and who to avoid. He
hadn't seen anyone he was entirely
drawn to but it was still early.
    "Rum and coke?" He queried the
bartend.
    "Sure thing." She chimed back. She
quickly mixed the drink. "We're out of
ice!" she hollered at some unknown
person.
    Harvey took his drink, acknowledged
the few men he recognized then found a
place in back where it was dark and
solitary. He didn't want to be alone.
Still, the solitary figures are the men
who eventually get hit on. Not the
overly talkative group members.
    An Australian gentleman who Harvey
had known at one time walked past
carrying a bucket.

"He must be the man with the ice."
Harvey thought.

Harvey's drink was too sweet. He
didn't much care for Rum and Coke. He
had only ordered it because he felt his
blood sugar was getting a bit low. It
was just a quick pick me up with a
little "chk".

Harvey hadn't expected to find a
great love of his life. I mean it had
been just too close to the strange
disappearance of his mother. He had
been out of sorts, had done a lot of
drugs. Had even hallucinated that his
own grandfather had fucked him. His
grandfather! A man Harvey had never
met, a man who was dead.

When Harvey finally met the man of
his dreams he had reduced his life to
an emotionless masterpiece. Life had
become an old black and white
photograph of Paris, Eiffel tower in
the background, in which he was the
only animated character. He spoke to
others, but even when they responded
all he heard was their silence and all
he remembered was their stillness and
hard angular features.

He had of course gotten deeply
involved with Jarren with whom he had
moved in. His old place had too much of
his mother and her mysterious
disappearance lying within it. He would

have gone crazy there, but perhaps he had gone a bit crazy anyhow.

Jarren had seemed patient and loving although those were entirely unreciprocated feelings. Harvey was numb and cold. Deep inside he missed the cities to the north. He wanted the filth and grime and missed his friends there. He felt like they had abandoned him when it was in reality he who had gone away.

Red Rob would have been a great comfort. He needed a hard-core pessimist like Red Rob to bring him around, not Jarren who fed him too much chipper, life is good bullshit.

"Shit though eloquently spoken, doth still fall from your mouth." Harvey had once read on a wall above the urinals in a public rest room. That was his perception of his best friend, Jarren, at the time.

Optimists are largely unappreciated.

Anyhow, that was what comprised a few years of Harvey's existence, with Jarren taking care of him all of the time while he wandered the city, blank and drunk, until the day he encountered a traveler, a sight see'er who seemed to come through the gray of Harvey's Parisian photo world with full color and animation.

The man in question was quite tall, roguish, and looked to be a man of many places. He wasn't well dressed, but was clean and had a confident sense of self. Something that Harvey felt he was lacking although the gentleman seemed to think Harvey was very self-identified. Harvey secretly hoped this was not the case. If this was really who he was then he felt there were much better people than he.

They met on a bridge, a very small one, in a park down town, city center, and there they sat and talked for hours. When the sun lowered the man invited Harvey to see a show. Harvey acquiesced.

The show was gaudy and ironic, and the audience was drawn into emotional participation with audio outbursts and sexually tilted comments. It was delightful since pomp and raunch are so rarely mixed with such carefully planned results. Harvey had silently given thanks to the thoughtfulness of the writers and directors in regard to the study of social atmosphere that was written into the performance.

After the movie the two had found a room in a local lodging house where they felt unobserved and after shyly removing the man's clothing, and sealing it away from the cleaners, they proceeded to make love.

They must have kissed every inch of each other, spending extra time on all

of the most forbidden places. Then they
made their way into the moment when
Harvey guided the man slowly inside
himself. He was careful because the man
was unusually thick and long.

Harvey groaned quietly as the man
kissed him and held him tight, pulling
Harvey strongly against him with every
heated thrust.

Harvey took long remembering looks
at the man's face in the low light,
memorizing the shape of his close
trimmed beard which he found incredibly
attractive. The motion of the mans
shoulders, in perfect rhythm with the
sliding and coming together of their
bodies stirred Harvey just as much as
the slick, driving, stirring motion of
the mans hard dick as it stroked
against the smooth inner walls of his
pink sex, and the thrusts were a
cushion of soft hair. The man's balls
were large and heavy, and hung
incredibly low as to bounce and slap
and tickle Harvey's buttocks with the
hair that thinly covered them.

The climax was extreme, and Harvey
curled his toes as the man let loose
hot jets of himself, injecting it deep
inside through a very rigid tool. The
kind of tool all men want to own.

Every exaggerated throb could be
felt between them as the man fell atop
Harvey, exhausted, and fell asleep

there inside him. Harvey felt content
for the first time in years, and also
fell asleep. Neither of them stirred
until the light of morning struck them
through the curtained windows and then
Harvey only stirred to switch places,
Harvey gently mounted and made love to
the man. Harvey realized afterward that
the spell that had been cast upon him
was lifted. He could feel again.

Harvey was brought briefly out of
his state of reminiscence by a puff of
cigarette smoke and music. The gent
with the Australian accent stepped up
behind him, squeezed his shoulder and,
perhaps sensing his loss of love, which
was so recent, had kissed him lightly
upon the left side of his ear just
above his ear. Harvey smiled. He
remembered the man, but not his name.
The gent didn't linger, just smiled
with understanding as he made his way
back to the front bar where he had been
seated earlier. With the man out of
sight Harvey picked up his drink and
headed to a table at the back bar.

The rest of the night was more or
less uneventful. Harvey had gone out
with the idea that he might like to get
lucky, but soon after he seated himself
at a table in the back.

He was joined by several annoying
and unattractive men who never left,
and drove away all of the good looking

and semi normal prospects. Harvey was too easy going to tell them to get lost. Instead he had another drink, and nodded politely while they bantered on drunkenly about whatever things made them feel important.

When Harvey left the bar, the world had taken on darkness. Not to say that he couldn't see, but more like there had always been an imperceptible light in the world, one that registered on an underlying conscious level, and that light had been dimmed. He was tense as he walked the gloomy Chicago street toward his hotel room. He wasn't sure exactly why he felt so anxious. Maybe it was just the alcohol, but he felt followed, watched.

Harvey wasn't exactly drunk, but when he reached his room he bolted the door, undressed in a haze, and as soon as his head hit the pillow, Harvey slept.

His dreams were fitful and incestuous. Flashing images of his imagined love affair with a long dead Grandfather beset him. There was no escaping them. Harvey tried to hide from them, but they found him anyway.

"Why have you left White City where I can protect you?" The dreams asked. "Where are you?

Chapter Ten

Past and Present

Mind Numbing Pain "Madam President?"

Anthony had grown so quickly, and it
seemed so fast to John. John worried
about the boy. There seemed to be no
room for emotional connection in the
boy. Anthony was a womanizer. He was on
to the next girl just as soon as he was
done fucking the previous. John was
still proud though. His little boy had
grown up with all of the family good
looks and then some. Maybe Sue had
contributed something to the marriage
after all, but John secretly blamed the
boys womanizing side on Sue's family.

John had been busy in his work back
in the lab. He was a very good inventor
and was very clever in the means he
used to protect his work from others.
He'd gotten an inquisition as to
weather or not he'd had anything to do
with the watchers. He was smart though
and wormed his way through it all.

He missed Tomm. The loss of love had
been tremendous. After he'd confronted
Tomm about stepping out they had argued

quite loudly, loud enough for Anthony
to hear. Tomm had left angry in the
middle of the night. John had thought
he'd be back. Anthony had come and
slept in the room with his father that
night. He'd been frightened twice that
night with the prospects of loosing his
family.

    "He's gone." John remembered the boy
crying. "And they will come for you
too."

    John had tried to reassure the
little boy, but nothing seemed to work.
His son had slept fitfully, mumbling
all night long.

    John hadn't slept. His guilt was
soaking through him. He had hurt the
two people he most loved that night.

    "When Tomm gets home I'll apologize
right away and never bring it up ever
again." He told himself.

    Tomm never came home though. John
spent the next month or so crying while
working in his lab all day. Anthony
stayed close at night, and John sent
him to stay with his friends and
relatives durring the day. Johns'
friends all supported him by helping
him care for Anthony in that respect.
They knew all too well the pain a
separation causes.

    Years had flown by like this, and
Anthony was no longer a little boy.

John spent most of that time inventing. The other John was in control while inventing, and most of it happened in a haze of mindlessness. There were quite a few little odds and ends that were lying around the lab, and he didn't even know what they did.

John was just feeling strong again when he had another run in with Sue. How he hadn't noticed her climb in power was beyond him. She had always been ambitious when it came to politics, and had crept into power as a nearly invisible underling. Well the President had a heart attack, and she had been his vice, it sounded ironic to John.

She had done her job as she had seen fit, and now that things had settled a little better she had some time to take care of personal effects. Her first move against John was vindictive. She came with a big bag full of lawyers and took Anthony. She froze Johns accounts calling him an enemy of the state. She felt that his inventions were a threat to the nations security.

John wasn't worried about the inventions. They were under lock and key of his own make. She couldn't have them. Were he to vanish they would simply sit forever and collect dust.

This was when the other John, the one who had slept, took real form. He

didn't cry. He was logical to a fault.
It was then that what John thought was
his other mind and he came together.

     Sue nimbly chewed at one of her
fingernails. She felt that things were
going very much to her liking. She had
finally gotten what she wanted most. It
was her rise to power that had been her
goal, at first that had been her
thought. Once it had been achieved she
hadn't felt in the least satiated
though. Instead she began having
nightmares.
     She dreamed relentlessly of a crying
baby and a rape that had happened so
long ago that she had believed the
memories lost and gone.
     She, of coarse, held her secret. She
had wanted it, needed it even. She had
been trying to drive him to it for
years. Through her entire marriage the
rape had been the only sex with John
that had been all about her. He had
only been looking at her, only thinking
about her. Even the slaps and punches
had meant he was only looking at her.
Not to mention the fact that other than
that night the sex had made her feel
guilty, even while they had done it.
     That night though, since it was
beyond her control, there had been no
guilt. She had been red and wet. Her
tits still tickled when she thought

about the first hard, penetrating
thrust. She had nearly gone inside out
with the feeling of him running through
her. It was fantasies of that night
that she had used during nearly every
sexual interlude with every other man
she had sex with since who could make
her orgasm. The only men who could make
her climax had been hard men, but never
harder than her. She had become a very
hard woman since. She liked her men up
behind her, rough chin against her neck
and shoulders.

   With all of this fantasizing going
on, why then did she feel this need to
bring John down? Where things different
she would have wanted him back but he
had lied to her. Sue hated knowing that
for all of those years with him, he had
wanted men like Tomm. Men, not women,
and had been fucking with Tomm while he
was with her, while she carried their
unborn son. What made it worse was that
John and Tomm had done so well, while
she had been left in a disheveled
state, and that Tomm had raised her
baby boy when it should have been her.
Not that she had really wanted to be a
mother anyway.

   Well Tomm was where he belonged.
Anthony was returned to her, and John
was now homeless and disheveled, all of
his former possessions now belonged to
her. Such were her thoughts when Chaz

entered her office. He was obviously flushed.

Sue liked seeing Chaz flushed. She eyed him lustfully. She made him stand uncomfortably, not addressing him. In his agitation he slipped up.

"Sue, we have a …"

"Silence!" She interrupted. He immediately assumed attention, straight faced, stone faced, remembering where he was and with whom.

Because he had broken protocol, and had used her first name, she made him stand much longer than normal just for effect.

"Yes?" She finally asked.

"Madam President." He said through his thick accent. "He is vanished and we are unable to enter his lab. His inventions remain under his control." Chaz was red in the face and was clearly unnerved in his failure to procure results to her demands. He had seen what the woman was capable of. He was so wound up that he flinched when Sue set her metal pen down on the desk with a tiny "click!" The muscles in his jaw tensed noticeably and his posture straightened as Sue began the rhythmic tapping of fingernails upon the lacquered surface of the desk. Although there was only a steely stare coming from Sue on the outside, on the inside she was smiling. She loved that she had

this kind of power over such a strong,
even militant man. She felt herself
growing moist, and underneath her desk
she crossed her legs and began bouncing
hre upper leg, a little known form of
pleasure for a woman, similar to
masturbation. The outside appearance,
however, was stern and was making Chaz
very nervous.

"*This is going to be fun.*" She
thought. Plan B was now in effect. Sue
had known it would be more difficult
than just walking in and taking it
away. John was a brilliant man, after
all.

"Meet me by the warehouse around
6:00 tonight." Sue said to Chaz. "Don't
be late." He nodded his acquiescence.

"Chaz?" She caught him on his way
out. "Bring a camcorder."

Chapter Eleven

In the Future

When God's Disagree

As is generally the case when two holy entities have a disagreement the result is unholy.

Because Mars had awakened, or rather not slept while Gia had slept far too deeply and for too long, he had a definite one up on her. Not to mention that his host body by chance happened to be pure genius without any alteration to his sentience. All things considered, at least Mars was aware of what it was the battle was really being fought over. He knew what the prize was. He'd had years to plot properly. His only real problem was that he couldn't control some of the pieces moving about the proverbial chessboard.

His host body was deteriorating too quickly and his newly chosen host had vanished. Sure there were others he could use. The bloodline he could use had broadened over the years while the bloodline Gia was dependent on had narrowed. His problem with the alternative hosts was that they were weak. It would take decades of wizard sleep to open one of them up to what he required of a host. If wizard sleep became necessary he would keep the host he already had with the same effect. He needed this new one in particular were he going to succeed in usurping this world and swapping it over for his stone, dust and dry planet.

Life is a precious commodity and it was exhausting to reach so far to find a host. At least he was closer to sentient life than the other Gods though.

Pluto, for instance, had a difficult time finding a host. Even the bloodline breed that had been made for him had no guarantee from that distance. Funny that considering the close proximity to her bloodline, Gia had run down to only one choice worth looking at. Then again so had Mars if he wished to get what he wanted.

Harvey had left his home in White City for only one reason. He discovered that he couldn't escape his former friends.

The pain of a lost love was small next to the pain of betrayal. Every time he saw either of them he remembered the good times with them, good times from which he was

specifically excluded. It was his fault
really. He had wanted his best friend
and his husband to be friends.
Somewhere in the mix they had become
such good friends with each other that
Harvey found he had simply been removed
from the activities. He was just a
third wheel.

When Harvey saw them together he was
hurt by three things the loss of love,
the loss of a best friend and the fact
that they had both betrayed him with
their lack of fidelity. He had trusted
them both to be there for him. Instead
he was alone. Since they had moved in
so close to where he himself lived they
were unavoidable, so Harvey left. He
went north where the climate would
match his mood.

Harvey woke up hard and horny. His
dick wanted a hole to stick. Harvey had
been here in this city before, and he
knew where to go. He threw on his
clothing in a rush and headed down town
to a local bar with a back room known
for sexual excess.

The back room was dark. It always
was. The fucking was hard and angry.
Harvey was on the edge of screaming his
rage as he with his hands on the hips
of the man bent over in front of him,
plowed the man's hole, balls to butt,
and came with all of the force he had
built up inside. The orgasm was long

and although he couldn't see the cum
shoot in long jets into the man who
grunted and took the load, he imagined
it shooting out of the round, red head
of his dick along with the rhythmic
shrinking and stretching of the veins
that ran through the length of it. He
grinned in the darkness at no one.

The man in front of Harvey struggled
to move away sensing the end of the ins
and outs of their frenzied encounter.
Harvey pulled hard on the man's hips
slamming his balls against the man's
buttocks, and slapped the man's ass
letting the man know that he had no
choice but to stay until Harvey was
done filling his hole with what he had.
He was standing in a bubble of
momentary comfort and when he was ready
he would break it and pull out, but not
before.

When he did pull out his dick was
wet, and semi hard. There was a
sucking, kissing sound with the exit as
the man, once anxious to get away, now
wanted the dick to stay.

Harvey was hungry though. He pushed
his dick back into his pants and left,
happy with the idea of the moisture
from the man's hole still coating his
dick.

The snow in Chicago was cold and
heavy. Each flake could have been a
crystal palace were you small enough to

appreciate them in such a light. Yet
all of the brightness made Harvey feel
somewhat diminished. Here he was, such
a small man in this dark, gloomy city
under a white sky. The city was teaming
with activity, none of it leisure. It
was very unlike White City where the
people were wealthy, and had been so
for generations.

Harvey had worked up quite an
appetite. He found a noisy but fairly
nice, out of the way café where the
food was well prepared. The service was
quite respectable and the price,
although not a concern for Harvey, was
reasonable. Harvey enjoyed his meal,
and dipped into dessert.

It must have been the chocolate
dessert, like a bad omen, just too much
of a good thing.

From the corner of Harvey's eye he
saw him, silver hair glinting at
Harvey. Startled Harvey looked up,
staring. He knew it was the man he had
convinced himself had never existed.
Harvey believed it was his Grandfather.
The man was sitting with an awkward
little woman. Feeling Harvey's eyes on
him, John looked up, and seeing Harvey,
he grinned. There was no mistake.

Harvey stood abruptly, and in the
time it took to blink the table where
he had seen the two of them sitting
stood empty.

A few of the other people who had come in to eat stopped dinning and stared at Harvey. Their little glow bugs winking at him as they swirled above the crowds.

Harvey, pretending to have a legitimate reason for jumping to his feet, headed for the men's room.

Was it just he or was there salt all over the seat where he had thought he saw his grandfather.

"Why am I hallucinating?" Harvey asked the air. "I haven't taken any strange chemicals."

Mars smiled, he had been only looking half-heartedly while he was sitting for dinner with another potential host.

She was a strange looking woman named Molly who had been very flattered that Mars had offered her dinner, believing he was interested in romance. Mars took her to a lousy little café in Chicago that he felt had very stale food. She seemed impressed though. She was one of his grandchildren, although she didn't know it. She was one of those who slipped through the cracks.

Her mother had passed on when she was young and she had never been curious about her father.

She had the power of his bloodline,
and Mars was considering her seriously
when he spotted Harvey.

Mars looked up for a better look and
smiled upon a very handsome grandson.
His timing was off, Harvey stood and
Mars evacuated dragging Molly along for
the ride.

Molly was panic stricken and
screaming. She had gone into hysterics
as Mars re-appeared within the deep
confines of his crystal cave, a place
known only to him and the other Gods.
They each had their own after a manner.

It had been the wrong place to go.
Gia was waiting for him. Molly it
appeared had a good reason for her
hysterics.

Mars found his power blocked. Molly
he saw was slowly being coated with
crystal, her screaming slowed and then
stopped, replaced with the drowsy sleep
like effect of the wizard sleep spell.

"How?" Mars gasped.

Of coarse Mars hadn't expected to
encounter any of the others, but he
knew Gia wasn't strong enough to keep
him from his power alone. He understood
when he saw the eagle that sat perched
next to her.

"Jupiter." He said.

Why Jupiter had come to Gia's aid
was beyond Mars. The eagle made sense.
Without a human host he had taken the

next best thing. In his case it was the eagle.

"I warned you not to cross me Mars." Gia chuckled. " You should have listened. I couldn't reach all of them, but I did manage a small council. We all feel you are too ambitious. We think you need a nap." Mars realized what was in store. He could feel the crystals forming on the tips of his hair already. Gia and Jupiter were forcing him into stasis. If he didn't break free now he wouldn't wake for centuries, maybe longer.

Mars hesitated, he had the strength to escape, but at such high cost. He even considered sleep for a moment. It had been a long time. The rest might even feel good. Then he realized that the price he would pay for his escape had a double edge. It would provide him with the ultimate revenge tool against Gia. At this point revenge would taste sweet. After all, he was Mars, God of war. Maybe it would teach her not to enter his home uninvited.

"No strength to flee Mars?" Gia chuckled in her airy light laugh, much like little bells.

Anger flooded through Mars then. "You've no idea what you've really done." Mars said to Jupiter. "Do not doubt that you have been mislead." He ignored Gia for the moment. He

remembered being her lover once, while
in a different host body. Lovers make
much more serious enemies when things
are turned and twisted around in the
right or wrong ways. Those who develop
enmity upon acquaintance rarely take
time to stalk each other across space
and time.

His mind had already begun to trace
through the necessary circuits for
escape. The connection he was making to
his giant crystalline world mind, where
Gods were born, took a moment of
complete concentration. He saw in his
mind what to a mortal would look as a
combination of paisleys somehow
combined with Mendel fractals. They
flashed across the backs of his eyes
like lightning. He knew this meant his
bloodline was lost, all but one. Well
two if you counted Molly, but then she
was in stasis now. Who knew how long
that would last before she woke?

Through the anger reflected in Gia's
eyes he could see a place where the
events that were transpiring would
later reflect pain and loss. She was
young and still didn't know the
loneliness of a dead world. His world
would live again eventually, but until
then he waited for sentience to find a
way to make base there.

Gia seemed to be intent upon
squelching the one thing her world had

that was worth coveting. Mars was calculated. He said the one thing that would cause her to lose all balance so he might run away. Even through the mind of his gay host he felt a momentary pang of desire for the woman and Goddess standing powerful and fierce before him.

"I love you, and I'm sorry for what is to come." He said as he looked into her dark eyes. She stepped quickly away from him as though he were a snake ready to strike.

As soon as her concentration wavered Mars felt the marrow in his bones burn as he bent all his will away from former God Spells, and instead focused on one single thought. He was going back to Chicago, and back to Harvey. Harvey would be the last strong host of his bloodline to survive the catastrophe to come. Mars hoped Harvey would help him.

It took all of his power to break free of the magical grip that lay upon him. His former God Spells would die with no fuel behind them. There would be no glow bugs, no watchers. The most horrifying thing was that without His connection to his first God Spell as John, White City would be no more. The entire city was made from salt that was spelled together. His red fire consumed him and he vanished.

"No!" Gia screamed. Jupiter leaped
into the air toward him, but Mars knew
that Jupiter was too slow to catch him,
even on wing. Mars appeared a moment
later outside of the men's room of the
café where he had seen Harvey. He could
feel that Harvey was inside so in Mars
stepped to encounter, and trust in
fate. It was all he had for the moment.

Chapter Twelve

Past and Present

Sue's Dark Secret

No one but Sue knew the dark depth
into which her soul could dive.

Chaz had shown up on time just as
she had planned, with camera.

Sue phoned in advance. The guards
should have all of the tedious work
done. She didn't want to waste any time
on knots, which she was terrible at
tying anyhow. Chaz, Sue noted, looked
much relieved that she hadn't shown up
with several cars full of thugs and
hired bodyguards. There were, of course
her Presidential escorts, but they
stayed back, and aloof.

This warehouse contained within it
one of Sue's biggest, and most
horrifying secrets. On the night that
Tomm had vanished, Sue had abducted
him. He had spent quite a number of
years locked up here. Sue had never
once seen him. She had been afraid of
what she might want to do to him were
he left in the same room with her.

She made arrangements that he be as comfortable as possible provided he remain hidden, and not leave the building. He was also never to be left unguarded or alone. Sue drove by the warehouse often, but had never gotten out of the car.

Tomm's living space was lavish. She knew because she paid the bills. She had swallowed her anger over credit card bills on several occasions only because were it up to her he would never see sunlight again, and it was up to her. Besides, the furniture was hers after all was said and done anyway, and the man had good taste. After all he had picked up her leftovers, meaning John.

Sue had thought of ordering Tomm's execution on a number of occasions, but had not committed to it. She felt that he would some day be of use to her. She'd been right. Tomm was the leverage she needed in order to unlock John's Lab, with all of its secrets.

Upon entrance, Sue found that she rather liked the furnishings she had purchased but never seen. There were no windows and the entire building was sound proofed. There were no walls within the living quarters. From any one camera all that there was to see could be seen.

Sue found Photo's of John and Anthony on the nightstand.

Books on various subjects littered the coffee table, which sat precariously far from the sofa.

Sue suddenly felt jealous of this man. She had never laid eyes on him. She had been afraid to look at the thing that she had been so callously tossed aside for, then replaced by. If he were ugly then she would be fierce because that would make her feel less than the angled, hard yet pretty woman she knew herself to be. Where he beautiful she would be inclined to change that for him.

"Skin deep they say about beauty, paper thin." She commented to herself.

"Ready?" Sue smirked crookedly at Chaz. Chaz wore a curious expression. He had no idea what Sue had planned. "Don't worry Chaz. All you have to do is hold the camera steady." Chaz grew visibly more relaxed.

Sue continued her course through the living quarters to the back room, which she knew would be ready. She hesitated for only a moment before she entered the cold dark room where she would confront a nightmare from her past. She fumbled for a moment looking for a light switch that when flipped ushered forth spotlights all pointed at the man

suspended between two wood posts by
thick rope and hard knots.

Chaz gasped and the door slammed
shut behind him.

Sue supposed she should have
expected the man to be nearly perfect.
Being locked in he had spent countless
hours using his workout equipment, *her
workout equipment*. Every muscle showed
in perfect detail. It appeared that the
guards had even taken the time to oil
him for the camera.

His skin was like white marble and
his black Italian hair gave stark
contrast to his skin. He had seen no
sun for nearly ten years, and his skin
was alabaster.

"Get that camera up and going!" Sue
snapped at Chaz who she noted was
standing loosely, obviously stunned.
Chaz jumped into motion, the camera up
and on his shoulder in seconds and
pointed toward the man bound,
suspended, naked.

"On me!" Sue commanded. Chaz obeyed.

"I have a message for you John." Sue
said to the camera, the man in the
background still faceless, nameless as
his back was turned to the camera. He
flinched and mumbled something angry
through the ball gag that held his
tongue.

"Don't be surprised. You should have guessed I had him all these years." Sue said as she began circling.

Chaz followed until Tomm's face came into view.

Sue walked to Tomm and squeezed his face from under his jaw, lifting his face and pushing her long manicured fingernails into Tom's unshaven cheeks.

Tomm shook his head in an attempt to break away from her touch and look away from the camera.

She immediately slapped him smartly across the face.

Tomm grunted.

Sue admired the red welt forming where her fingers had fallen.

"I have two reasons for doing this little video message." Sue began as she now gently ran the backs of her fingers downward across Tomm's face, neck, chest and stomach messing and teasing the dark hair that grew there.

"One is that I want you to witness me doing to him the equivalent of what you did to me on the night I left you. Dear, sweet revenge…" Sue smiled. "And second, I want the inventions in your lab and any others you might think up later."

Sue smiled into the camera calmly as she smoothly doubled up her fist, then looking away from the camera swung it solidly into Tomm's stomach. He grunted

audibly and coughed through his gag
blowing spittle through his nose, as
his mouth was sealed shut.

Sue pulled a couple of hair needles
from her hair, and tossed her head to
let her hair fall from the tight knot
she wore it in and took off her suit
coat. The suit coat she tossed to the
floor behind her.

"This is a mild example of what I
will do if you don't give me what I
want." She placed first needle against
Tomm's bicep where it was upraised by
the position in which he had been tied.
He was tied tight and had no room to
move away. Only the fear in his eyes
showed how Tomm felt as Sue drove the
needle through his arm, straight
through muscle.

"Look how clean?" She commented "No
Blood?" Tomm was shaking, the pain
already getting to him.

"Don't assume that showing this
video to anyone will get me into any
trouble." Sue said. "After the week is
out, you'll know why." She said as she
stepped to a small table that had lain
unnoticed before. She set down the
second hair needle and picked up a long
black nightstick. Sue quickly
calculated where the blow would land.
She didn't want to worry about medical
care so she needed to strike where it
would hurt badly but cause no real

damage other than heavy bruising. She
stepped to Tomm's side and smiled into
the camera, raised her arm for the
swing then looked to the target. It
struck full force across the tendons on
the back of his knees.

This time Tomm's noise wasn't a
grunt, but a muffled cry. He'd closed
his eyes tightly as shaking consumed
him. Sue found it interesting how
quickly a man's strength could be
removed. He wouldn't walk for over a
week.

"Does it hurt?" Sue said with mock
sympathy dramatically pushing out a
pouting lip. "I just have two more
things for you. It won't be long, and
as long as Johnny comes through with
what I want, you'll never have to see
me again." She stepped to the table to
set down the nightstick. "I'm a little
disappointed. I had wanted a longer
session, but I can see you won't be
able to handle it. Your just a weak
little man."

"Get a good shot from his front!"
Sue snapped at Chaz. "I want John to
see the look on his face for this one."
Tomm couldn't see the massive dildo Sue
carried behind him from the table.

Chaz flinched a little shaking the
camera momentarily.

Sue reached up to the back of Tomm's head and deftly untied the knot holding the gag then pulled it free.

"You filthy bitch!" Tomm immediately spat.

"Composure Tomm," Sue smiled. "But then I do so care about what you have to say to me." She said as she stood invisibly rubbing lubricant onto the dildo then, without warning, pushed all of her weight into it, shoving the dildo into his unprepared anus.

The scream that came from Tomm could only be defined as maddened. Chaz nearly dropped the camera.

Sue, unflinching let go of the dildo, which dropped to the floor amongst another scream.

Tomm continued screaming and was now sweating and shaking uncontrollably. Sue knew she had accomplished what she had set out for. She knew that John would give her what she wanted.

"Close up on the face now dear." She purred at Chaz.

He obeyed over quick, obviously afraid.

Sue stepped to the table one last time and lit a candle. She was holding something over it running it back and forth, a brand of some sort.

"I know that you're a clever man John. So this last little thing is so that if you manage some miraculous recovery and escape with your little queer lover, you will never be able to make love to him without thinking of me."

Sue paused and held the brand in front of the camera. It glowed angry and red.

"It says Suzy, for me." She said pertly. "And Q for filthy little queer!" She spit through pursed lips. Then pressed it into Tomm's cheek.

It hissed. Smoke curled into the air and Tomm screamed again though it was more broken crying than screaming now. Sue pulled the brand away. She noted that it stuck just a little. "See there? Suzy Q..." It shone black on Tomm's white cheek. Sue motioned the camera to her.

"John," she smiled. "I'll give you one month to come through then me and Tomm will become properly acquainted." She motioned the camera off.

"Guard!" she commanded.

A man appeared startling Chaz. Chaz was military trained, but he'd had no idea the man had been there.

"Clean Tomm up and make him comfortable. He's had a bad day." With that she walked out. Chaz followed.

"I'll need that video now Chaz." Sue said.

"Yes Madam President!" Chaz said formally, ejecting the tape and handing it to her.

"Go wait for me at the car."

"Yes Madam..." Sue's hand shot up cutting him off from any further conversation.

On the sofa sat a dark haired man of South American decent. He stood to greet the president as she approached.

As soon as Chaz was out of the building they sat. Tea had been made. Sue poured herself a cup and smiled at the man.

"You've found him I assume?" She said.

"I have." He said.

"You are amazing..." Sue cajoled. "Will you deliver this to him along with what ever he will need in order to view it?" She asked politely.

"By your request alone my lady." The man smiled. She placed her hand on the man's leg.

"Thank you." She took a sip of tea.

"Thank you."

Chapter Thirteen

In the Future

Mars

The waitress had thought the man at table 13 attractive. He was dark, and seemed a to pout a little. She liked men who needed her to entertain them. She had, however, been a bit alarmed when he jumped out of his seat and looked frantically around the room as though he had seen a ghost, She didn't like the paranormal. Then the man had just walked to the men's room. The waitress thought nothing more of it.

Harvey was just shaking it off after a good piss when John stepped into the men's room.

Harvey zipped up so fast that he narrowly missed getting it caught in the line up.

"Hello Harvey." His grandfather smiled at him.

Harvey didn't know what to say. He stood stunned. He didn't need to say anything though because it was that moment that Mars collapsed. Harvey caught the man roughly.

The waitress seemed to have been waiting for them when Harvey stumbled out of the restroom into the restaraunt bearing the weight of the man in his arms. Without hesitation she helped them to the table where Harvey had been seated and together they sat Mars into a chair.

"Could you bring me a sandwich please? I haven't eaten in a while and that's all that's wrong." The waitress stood looking much relieved at the simple explanation and hurried off to get the order.

"I thought you were a dream," Harvey said, not knowing where to begin.

"I'll explain later." Mars said. "I need you to take us somewhere safe where we can be alone."

"What?" Harvey asked, confused.

"Just trust me on this. The world you know is about to fall apart. I built it, and I know what it rests on and that foundation is crumbling as we speak."

Harvey didn't understand, but was astute enough to know that he wouldn't get an explanation here and now.

The sandwich had arrived, and Harvey watched as this man, his strangely immortal grandfather ate as though he had never eaten before. Then it began. Harvey could hear gasps from the other patrons of the café.

"What's going on?" Intoning his question to his grandfather. Mars simply motioned Harvey's attention to one of the many viewer screens that sat motionless around the café. White City was crumbling and sinking into the ocean. Not only was it crumbling, it was literally falling to powder, turning into fine salt and dissolving into the ocean. The only people who would have a chance to escape would be the ones on the border of the city facing the mainland, and it would take a damn good swimmer to make it that far with the rip tides and undertow.

Chapter Fourteen

Past and Present

Bait the Hook. Catch the Fish.

John knew they would search for him.
The other him had warned that he hadn't
really lost them, at least not all of
them. So it was really no surprise to
him when the package arrived.

"No return address." John mumbled to
himself. "What a surprise." The other
John was much more integrated now.
Together they had become one very
articulate individual. Still there were
secrets that the other was withholding
from John. The time wasn't right to
reveal it all. John didn't press. He
knew that whatever the truth was he
wasn't quite ready for it. He was a
smart man and was aware that the other,
although it appeared as if it were him
in dreams, was alien. Still, John had
struck a bargain with it and he was
going to live up to his end of it.
After all the other had lived up to all
of it's obligations, never once telling
lies.

John opened the plump, bubble-lined envelope. Inside he found a new laptop computer and a disc. He put the laptop down. What he didn't know couldn't hurt him. Still the events of the last month showed that Sue was one of the most diabolical tyrants of all time. It was obviously something she had been planning for a long time, this message she had sent.

John had handed her the world. Using his formulae to create impenetrable fabric she had garbed an army in armor that no bullet could pierce. In one month she had simply seized control of every country on the planet. Those who resisted soon found that all they could do was watch their armies die. Her personal list of new laws was due out in four months. Any guilty parties could look forward to immediate imprisonment. Any who resisted were looking at immediate execution. No one but John knew enough about the woman to know what that meant. During her political career she had kept her views quite hidden.

The general public wasn't in a state of panic however, but rather one of relief. They adored her. After all, she was pretty, strong, smart and the world was hers.

"It was about time someone did something!" was a commonly heard sentiment.

Ignorance is bliss. The public smiled at the storm. Troops could now be found on every street corner, in their shiny white armor. The soldiers smiled and preened, not knowing themselves what they could be commanded to do. After three months of priming their egos with power, few would refuse whatever command they were given.

The prison camps had been built in secret, years in advance. Instead of outrage at their appearance there was neutrality due to the fact that they wouldn't strain the economy. The almighty dollar still ruled.

John started to walk away from the damn computer.

"Watch it." The other warned.

"It'll mean nothing but trouble." John replied.

"I'm older than you can imagine. Knowledge is power. Not knowing will mean more trouble."

"As you wish."

John looked back to the cursed computer, picked it up, and opened it. He powered it up and put in the disc. He was horrified.

John was doubly horrified because he felt responsible. He had really let himself believe that Tomm had simply

left him. Not once had he thought to
track him down. He had believed what
others had told him.

"If you love him let him go." He'd
been told. "If he comes back then you
will know it was meant to be." His
friends had warned.

John had been heartsick with the
betrayal of being abandoned. Now he was
heartsick with the fact thrown in his
face that he had not been abandoned,
but had in truth abandoned his love to
fate and worse. His lover hadn't left
him, but had been taken from him.

"I have to go to him." John thought.

"Don't go. There is another way."
The other contradicted.

"I'm going to him!" John argued.

John was crying. The salty tears
burned more than they should have. John
knew it, felt it. His Tomm was being
tortured because he hadn't been
watchful, because he hadn't guarded his
family.

*"I won't force your hand. I promised
you that, but if you give yourself to
this woman, this creature, I won't go
with you. I can't let you make the same
mistake twice."*

The tears falling from John's eyes
were fire. As they hit the ground they
glowed ugly and red. The pain was quite
real.

"What are you doing to me? John asked aloud as the pain blinded him and the world became darkness.

"*I'm leaving you.*" John heard the other as though it were spoken from very far away. "*Your sight will return.*"

"Why do you leave?" John cried.

"*I told you. I won't let this mistake happen again. I have a thing to do.*"

"What?"

"*It's called a God Spell.*"

John was muddled of mind as the knowledge lent to him by the other burned out of him, and blind, he never saw the puddle of his own tears become the first glow bug. It was born of his need to protect Tomm and even the world from Sue who had become a great evil. It flew away along with the other, leaving John alone to his confusion.

Tomm was reading when the little ball of glowing stuff first appeared next to his right ear. He swatted at it a few times and was a little amazed at how rapidly it moved out of his reach. It hovered antagonistically on the edge of his vision. It was a little weird. He thought that maybe it was like a spot you get from looking at a light too long. He tried going back to his reading.

"It moved, it definitely moved." He thought.

Tomm closed his book and turned his head to get a closer look. This time it stayed put. Apparently comfortable with being viewed now. Whatever it was it was contrived. Possibly made by a human hand.

Tomm took more interest. He wanted a closer look, but when he leaned toward it, it moved away. He tried to catch it and it moved away even further. Only a moment after he put his hand down it returned.

It seemed sentient. Still it was antagonizing to him.

His recovery had been painful, and he was still stiff and sore, but he was mobile. He grabbed the nearest book to swing at the thing. He was immediately met with a headache. He felt it had something to do with his attempt to swat the little bug down. As soon as he set the book down it returned to its original position and the headache left.

"Perhaps it's another guarding device, set to watch me." Tomm thought. It would be no surprise, especially now that he knew who held him captive.

For years he hadn't had the faintest idea who was holding him captive, or what their motive was. Any attempt to

press the guards for information
resulted in severe beatings.

A man came once a week to do a
grocery list. That was the extent of
communication he was allowed. He
discovered quickly that the amount of
money spent wasn't a concern

He'd been raped a few times by the
guards. They made sure he didn't enjoy
it. He learned quickly that it wasn't
the sex that turned these men on, but
his humiliation, pain and submission.
He supposed he should feel grateful for
the rapes now. What they had done to
him had readied him for what that bitch
had done, otherwise having that monster
dildo shoved up his ass would have done
irreparable damage. His ass still hurt
though. Taking a dump was very
uncomfortable.

John turned himself in shortly after
the other had left him. It seemed that
the guards he had gone to had been
expecting him. They had known right
where to find him.

Without hesitation he had been put
on a plane, and flown to wherever it
was his quiet little cell had awaited
him. He had no idea where that might be
as he'd had a bag over his head the
whole time. There was no way to
landmark anything. The place was too
private to be a prison. John was quite

nervous. He realized now that he hadn't
helped Tomm in the least. If anything
he had doomed him by allowing himself
to be captured.

Sue had come to the same conclusion
quickly. She was tired of the man
sucking up her money, and she wasn't
about to let him go. He wasn't
dangerous, but he was, well, let's just
call him a loose end. She wanted it
tied off.

She passed a little sealed note to
Chaz and told him to take it to the
warehouse. Chaz silently complied.
Later that day Chaz delivered the
message then left. He didn't ever want
to see the place again. Images of that
evening when he had stood holding that
damnable camera haunted him. The
screams he heard in his dreams, he
found to be his own upon waking.

Sue, who he had once found pretty,
now terrified him. He was so horrified
of her that he didn't even dare let on
that he had been bothered. He wanted a
transfer, but putting in for one now
would make his discomfort obvious, and
Sue was a woman that he didn't want to
piss off.

Her notes appeared, on the outside,
to be sweet love letters. The man who
received it thought as he accepted it.

He waited for the deliveryman to leave
before he opened it, breaking the
little heart shaped seal. She was a
deeply deceitful woman, which he
appreciated. He was a big fan. He noted
the lavender scent that somehow matched
the blue paper and read the words that
were printed in a rather flowery hand.

"Kill Him!" It practically smiled.

He did smile.

Jason was his name, and Sue had
found him amongst a group of sadist
years earlier. He remembered the others
in the group always warning about
knowing when and where to stop. He had
never wanted to stop. He didn't want
any boundaries.

When Jason thought about it all now
he was sure it was the warnings from
the others in the group that had
brought her to him. He had thought her
a foolish young thing at the time. She
had invited him to a dinner at her
home. He had thought seriously about
where he might hide her body were he to
go too far.

Jason, like Sue's note, was not what
he seemed. He had smooth, pale skin,
strawberry blond hair, dashing blue
eyes and a smile that emanated
innocence. Women had thrown themselves
into his arms his entire life. All of
them would have regretted it had they
lived long enough. Looking at Jason, a

person would never guess what he was
capable of.

He remembered Sue's house. On the
outside it was quite pretty. Pale pink
paint and white shutters, soft rows of
petunias bordering the walk. He had
thought upon his approach that it would
be too easy. He had been very wrong.

He knocked, and she answered
immediately. He had barely stepped
through the door when he was attacked
and securely held by two very large
guards. He, it appeared, had been the
sucker, suckered in by her.

On the inside it wasn't even a
house. He was hauled into a center room
where there were no windows and where
it had been sound proofed. He hadn't
bothered making any noise, nor did he
bother struggling. He was tied to a
post with his hands over his head in
seconds, and left to her.

"What did you want to do to me?"
She'd smiled into his blue eyes.

"I'd planned to torture you then
bury you somewhere." Jason had said
quite honestly. She pulled a knife out
of her back pocket. Slowly she used it
to pull buttons off of his shirt, and
then she ran the point of it down his
now bare and smooth chest.

"An eye for an eye." She'd said as
she popped the top button off of his
pants. He didn't panic. "You're a hard

man." She'd continued as she undid his zipper pulling free his rather small dick. "Not much to look at here." She'd said, tickling it with her fingertips. He frowned. "I have a job for you, but I think I'll train you up a bit first."

"If I refuse?" Jason questioned… She immediately grabbed his balls and squeezed hard. He grunted thinking to outlast her. She simply continued to squeeze until his baby blue's rolled back into his head.

"You don't have a choice anymore slave." She'd said as she released her grip.

"You won't break me you bitch!" He said low, growling…

"We have time to find out." She leaned in and whispered into his ear, nonchalant.

"My friends in the group know where I am. They'll know if I disappear." Jason gritted his teeth. He hated being helpless.

"I own the group. Your friends broke very easily. You and I have a lot of time." She stepped back and turned to leave. "Drug him." He heard her say as she left the room. "Do what you want with him, but he stays tied where he is, and absolutely no bruises. I want to make those myself."

"Yes madam!" The guards said in unison.

Jason had taken two years to break.
The first week was spent tied to that
damn post. Sue drugged him just to
watch him withdrawal until he begged
her for his fix. She beat him. She
raped him. She fed him. She loved him.
She killed his self-identity so many
times that he finally stopped creating
new ones. When she felt he was ready,
she cleaned him up, stopped drugging
him and made sure he wouldn't be an
addict when he was left to his own
devices. Then she finally came to him
and gave him the most intense, violent
sex he had ever had. He was no longer a
homicidal maniac, or a murderer. Now he
was a killer. He killed without mercy
or guilt, and only at her request. He
doubted he would enjoy it without her
request.

Jason became a high-ranking officer
in what he found later was Sue's own
personal army. Her men and women were
everywhere. Jason had loved Sue's
attention and he'd had her attention
until this misfit appeared. He resented
this assignment. No visible bruises and
no permanent damage had been her
orders. Anything else went.

Jason had never touched the man with
his own tiny prick but he'd done every
other mean sexual indignity he could
imagine to the man. He'd even shoved
his own hand up the man's ass. He'd

made sure it would hurt. Now he could
finally off the motherfucker and he
wanted it done now. He was ready for a
new assignment.

He entered the man's quarters and
found the man napping peacefully on the
bed. Jason wasn't interested in
torture. He just wanted to be done with
it. He pulled out his gun, pointed and
began to slowly squeeze the trigger.

His finger froze. He inhaled sharply
and tried to squeeze. His hand locked
up, and to his dismay his arm lowered.
A little ball of glowing light caught
Jason's attention. He grunted fighting
to raise his arm for the kill.

Tomm rolled over awakened by Jason's
grunt. Finding a gun pointed in his
general direction he jumped to move out
of the way. The little lightning bug
flashed with a blaze of light much like
a flash bulb. The gun fired into the
empty mattress then fell to the floor.

Jason's fingers felt like they were
on fire when what could only be
described as a feeling like being shot
in the head overtook him. He screamed
and fell over.

*"If I've been shot in the head
shouldn't I be dead."* Jason thought to
himself. Instead his eyes were locked
open. Pain throbbed and shot through
him. Jason couldn't escape the pain
right to the day he finally died which

was only a few weeks later. An eye for
an eye, he'd intended to shoot a man in
the head, and was left with the pain of
being shot in the head, until it killed
him.

Tomm watched, shocked as this guard
choked and writhed on the floor, then
the little glow bug came back to hover
over his head like a little guard. Tomm
suddenly understood it. He had known
John was a brilliant inventor. He
assumed that this little bug was
another of John's inventions.

Tomm wasted no time. He went through
the guard's pockets and pulled the
keys. He would make his run for it. He
pulled on some clothes and shoes then
made for the door. The moment he went
through the door two guards went down
clutching their arms as though broken.
Tomm kept moving, the glow bug
flickering just to the side of his
sight. Within minutes he was out of the
building leaving over forty guards
incapacitated, some in pain, others
simply unconscious. Into the city he
fled. For a moment he worried that the
glow bug would attack anyone he
encountered. He soon discovered,
however, that it incapacitated only
those who sought to injure him. Tomm
breathed the free air, and for the
first time in years, he genuinely
smiled.

"Thanks John my love." He said to
the sky. "Thanks."

Sue decided not to wait. She signed
the form to have all sexual deviants
arrested and sent to her camps. She'd
had their names for years so it was
just a matter of picking them up. The
internet had made her list so easy.
Even in foreign countries the lists
were quite complete. Hookers, queers,
adulterers all should be arrested
within the week. Sure there would be
fewer mail men and the house wives who
seduced them, for a while, but the
world would thank her some day. She was
sure of it. She hadn't left out drug
dealers and junkies, but they were
better in pharmaceutical schools or
inpatient care. They were victims, not
criminals. She'd get around to that
later though. John's little crab shaped
spies were nearly everywhere, and she
could find every lawbreaker with ease.
   Sue was just getting ready to pat
herself on the back for her good deeds
when there was a tap on the door. Sue
frowned.
   "Never a moments peace." She
grumbled. "Enter!" She commanded. The
door opened and Chaz entered the office
and stood at attention to the side of
the door letting it close with a nearly
inaudible click.

"Yes Chaz?" Sue questioned. She
realized now that she had gone too far
with the man. He was no longer aroused
in her company. She had apparently
misjudged what the man was into. She
thought briefly about slave training,
but he would be missed. Besides, she
was loosing interest in him anyway.
She'd probably just can him and be done
with it.

"We've captured John, your husband,
He's in a cell downstairs as we speak."
Chaz said.

Sue's smile was genuine. She had
thought of a thousand uses for John.
The main one was fixing the Gay
problem. She was sure they could be
fixed since there was obviously
something wrong with them. John was an
inventor, and she wanted to see what he
was capable of. She still hated him,
but he was a valuable resource. Sue's
nipples rose against her shirt.

"Take me to him." She commanded.

John was staring at the slit of
light filtering under the door to his
cell when it hit him that he wasn't
smarter than the average man, but that
his ego had led him to believe himself
smarter. None of the inventions he'd
made were really his. They all had
belonged to the other. The desire for
the things, or the need of them was

always his, but the mind bending had
always been the other.

A shadow fluttered across the floor
on the other side of the door. There
was a loud "click" as it was unlocked,
then two guards entered. Behind them
entered Sue.

"Hold him!" She commanded the
guards. They immediately lifted him up,
one on each arm. Leaving the door open
Sue crossed the room and slapped him
smartly.

"I've wanted to do that for years."
Sue said.

"What do you want Sue?" John said.
He realized that the slap had made his
lip bleed. He hadn't tasted his own
blood for some time. Not since the
other had come to be with him really,
and now he was alone again, and
apparently more vulnerable.

The room seemed a little warm all of
a sudden.

"What will you give for his
freedom?" Sue asked cleverly. Looking
at her ex husband had awakened
something inside her womb. She was
remembering that night when he had
taken her. She wanted that from him.
She knew it wasn't likely, but she was
a patient woman.

"I'll give whatever is in my power
to give." He said, and meant. He could
see no other way around the situation.

"I'll let him go if you mean that."
Sue lied. She knew that Tomm probably
lay in a pool of his own blood by now.

The room seemed unusually hot to
her.

"Thank you." John said although he
felt it had been too easy.

"It won't be easy." Sue said.
"You'll still never see him again, and
should opportunity to see him come to
you, you'll have to deny him." John's
suspicions were awakened and then again
settled.

"What specifically do you want of
me?" John queried. Sue waved the men
off of John. He was no threat.

"Bring some decent chairs in here!"
She commanded the guards. "I want your
inventions." She redirected to John.

The guards returned with a few
wheeled office chairs for the two to
sit on. "Please sit." Sue motioned John
to a chair. *He is still very
handsome.*" She thought to herself.

"Okay." John said. He couldn't
remember anything about them, but he
believed that it would return to him
eventually. "You said as much in your
message…" Silence struck the room for a
moment.

Sue unbuttoned the top button of her
blouse. It was hot in here.

"The message was extreme, I admit,
but would anything less have got you

here? I promise he's been taken care
of." Sue said. It was no lie as she
felt that his death definitely took
care of him.

"What else?" John asked again.

"Marry me!" Sue said.

John was both flabbergasted and
angry.

"Marry you!" He yelled. "After what
you did!" Guards immediately showed at
the door. Sue waved them away. John was
gripping the armrests of the chair so
tightly now that his knuckles were
white.

"After what you did to me?" Sue
said, and laughed at him. Her laugh was
like cursed wind chimes. John was now
looking around nervously, looking for
an escape. Sue loved watching a big
strong man squirm. She definitely
didn't love him. She did want him
though. She wanted to own him, body and
soul. Her goal was within her reach.

"You remember what you did to me
right? It's been about 17 years now?"
John looked away from her guilty of
what she accused.

"Why marriage?" He said, seemingly
to the wall. He couldn't look at her.

"Our son needs a father, and won't
even speak to me. If you marry me he
will grow to trust me. He's here you
know." John's eyes watered at the
mention of Anthony. "You won't have to

sleep with me for god's sake John!" Sue
piped. Just make it look good for him
and the camera's"

"It's pure foppery!" John retorted.

"Politics is always pure foppery
John. It's for the best."

"Says who?" John was on the edge of
screaming again. "You?"

*Sue was so calm, Why was she so calm
Damn it?* He thought.

"It would also be nice if you could
get control of your little spy
cameras." Sue reminded him. "They are
troublesome and are popping up in
cities across the world. One might
question where that will end."

"I won't marry you!" John said
adamantly.

Chaz appeared unexpectedly in the
doorway looking flustered. He was
sweating.

"Goodness." Sue stirred looking
flustered. It was obviously for show.
"A woman's job is never done." She said
standing and heading for the door.
"Think it over a while John. After all,
it beats the alternative you know. This
cell for the rest of your life for
instance?" She ushered the guards out
of her way and left with Chaz on her
heels. The door closed and locked with
a loud "click."

As soon as she was gone John threw a chair at the door. It hit with a very loud crash. The room was roasting.

"Yes Chaz?" Sue asked. She was feeling very happy.

"Tomm has escaped." Chaz informed her.

"What???" Sue screamed. She was rarely taken so off guard and totally lost composure. "Where the hell is Jason?"

"He's in the hospital." Chaz answered, trying not to flinch under her extreme fury. "As are all the other guards from the facility." Sue stopped in her tracks.

"John!" She said as if it were the answer to everything. "I'll kill him!" She turned on her heels and headed back toward John's cell.

John sat on his cot wondering if she weren't right. The alternatives looked bad for him and there was Tomm's freedom at stake. He was about to go knock for a guard and acquiesce when his cot burst into flame. The sprinkler system for fire control sprang into action and to John's surprise he was confronted with himself, only he was comprised of red flame. It was the other.

"I've taken care of Tomm." John's fire composed reflection hissed at him crackling through the water droplets. The room was blistering. "Are you ready to come with me?"

"To where?" John asked himself, wondering why he even questioned under the circumstances. The questions seemed formal, instinctual, predetermined even.

"To your destiny. I must warn you that I can't go back into your mind like I was. If you come you will have to integrate with me completely."

"What does it entail?"

"I'm symbiotic. It will hurt a lot at first. Then you'll like it, very much probably. You'll be much smarter and there are other benefits."

"And the cost?" John asked.

"We will never speak like this again. We will become one mind, neither you nor me but both."

John held out his hand nervously and the other touched it. Flesh burned but didn't blister then the other stepped into him like walking into a mirror. Everything felt like a sunburn slap. John's mind felt like an electric storm. He was washed away, and then reborn. His memories looked through history like a giant book for an explanation. He remembered forever. He felt outer space around him, and

although his heart still beat he knew
that there was another heart, far away
on another world. A whole planet pulsed
inside him. He found the answer in
folklore. He was Mars, and that is
where he went, leaving the cell in
flames that quickly died, hissing in
the water from the sprinklers.

Sue burst into the cell, screaming
at the guard for being too slow opening
the door. Her hair had fallen out of
its tight knot on top of her head and
she was soaked. Inside the cell she
found nothing but burnt furniture.

"No!" She screamed in fury. First
she stood staring at the empty room,
shaking. Then she was shaking from the
cold water. Chaz gently took her by the
elbow, and led her from the cell to
where she could dry off. She was silent
and pursed lipped. She was thinking,
planning.

Chapter Fifteen

In the Future

Salt

Harvey knew it was more than a
little weird. I mean how could a man
who was over 100 years old still be so
attractive. Not to mention the fact
that the man was his grandfather. He
had made love to his grandfather, and
when it came down to it he hadn't felt
incestuous, but vindicated. His
thousands of half brothers and half
sisters never really felt like family.
They felt like a bunch of country club
snobs who he had mistakenly fallen in
with. Not to mention the fact that
anyone in White City who fucked anyone
else could be a half brother or half
sister with his or her partner. His
long dead father had sired thousands.
All of them moved to White City, and
had lived there until moments ago.
    Harvey had a rather large number of
questions for this silver haired man,
but he held his tongue. None of them
could be asked here without being

overheard. So he did as he was asked
without questioning.

He remembered this man on his arm
being much stronger. The man's robust
form appeared a bit diminished. He was
thinner, and definitely at a loss for
strength. The blood sugar line was
bullshit. Harvey had seen the man
dining with a woman only moments
earlier. Still he guided the old man
down the street to his hotel room.

As soon as the two were inside and
the door was closed John collapsed onto
the bed and passed out. Harvey, having
grown accustomed to cleaning up fucked
up bar types when they had out done
themselves calmly undressed the
sleeping man leaving only his boxers,
which Harvey noted were made of fine
silk, and gently rolled the man under
the covers and tucked a pillow under
his head. He took a moment to check a
temperature with the back of his hand
then the pulse and breathing. He didn't
want the old man to kick it or
anything. Harvey needed information.
Everything seemed normal. Harvey noted
that there was no glow bug with the
man. He thought it was strange but it
explained how he had seen his mother
slap the man. Harvey knew that this man
knew what had happened to his mother.
These two seemed to be Harvey's only
real family members. He was torn

between anger and concern. He took a seat in the hotel chair and watched the man rest.

"You haven't lost your looks for your age." Harvey spoke to the stale air. The man stirred but quickly went back to sleep.

Harvey may have sat there like that for hours when his own glow bug flickered. It caught his eye and he looked to it. It flashed one more time then fell to the floor. No more light emanated from it.

Startled Harvey stood to investigate. He found only a little pile of powder. He touched it to see what it was. He couldn't tell by looking. He tasted it.

"Salt." He said aloud.

"Yes, Salt." Harvey jumped at the sound of another voice. He hadn't realized that the man had woken. Harvey couldn't help staring at him. John was sitting on the edge of the bed where his balls could hang low enough to settle onto the mattress. His body was rock solid and silver hair grew only where it accentuated his masculinity. His boxers had been casually removed at some point during his rest.

"It appears to be over." Mars said. "No more protection for the innocent."

"Would you mind explaining to me what's going on? Grandfather…" Harvey

tried the word out. It sounded wrong
somehow. The man furrowed his brow,
looked antagonized and at the same time
deeply injured.

"Call me John. It's what all my
lovers have called me, all but one."

"But I am aren't I, your grandson?"

"Yes."

"You've managed to avoid my
question. Are you going to vanish again
without any explanation?" Harvey was
bold. It wasn't in his nature to show
fear. He had really never felt it. The
mystery of this man would scare most.

"It's a long and complicated story."

"I have time." Harvey said taking
his seat again.

"Not enough for it all." John said.

"You could start with my mother."
Harvey said with a little bit of an
edge. John sighed with frustration. He
admired Harvey's strength of will.
Harvey would be his strongest host yet.

"That's an emotional tale. I hope
you won't mind if I avoid it for a
little longer."

"She is the only family I've had.
I've lost her and I want her back. I
have a good strong feeling you know
where to find her."

"My boy I have just lost nearly
every grandchild I have in that sunken
city. There is now only yourself and
one other, and she is in a good deal of

trouble. I'm no stranger to loss. Have
patience. In time I'll give you the
entire story. As I said, it's
complicated. I have to start with the
basics. You are part of a much stranger
family than you realize. Besides I
think the story can wait for me to take
a shower."

John stood without waiting for an
answer.

Harvey looked without hesitation. It
was exactly what he remembered. He
wished it had been part of the genetic
line he had inherited. It was as large
as Harvey's own now erect dick, yet it
was not erect. It bounced before Harvey
for only a moment as John headed for
the shower.

Harvey adjusted himself. This would
be hard. Harvey admired the triangle of
hair on John's lower back just above
his buttocks as the man walked toward
the shower, soft, perfectly shaped.

Harvey listened to the sounds
outside change while he watched the
steam flow over the top of the shower
curtain. His imagination was admiring
the man behind it. By the time the
curtain opened He was as erect as he
had ever been. He wanted to pull out
his dick and jack off right then and
there, but was torn.

John seemed oblivious to Harvey's
desire. He slowly pulled the towel

across his chest and belly hair then
rubbed it over and around his rather
large dick and balls, the power of
touch making it momentarily charged,
but not erect.

Harvey licked his lips.

John put back on his boxers and
proceeded on toward his clothes that
were laid out on the other chair.

Harvey hated to see the man dressed
again, yet it would take some time for
him to settle down enough to stand
without being obvious.

Chicago had been busting for a
while, overly loud and busier than
normal. Now it was silent. Harvey
remembered the shock and dismay from
the people in the café as they had
watched White City crumble.

"Maybe you would start with the
salt?" Harvey asked.

"That is perhaps the most
appropriate place to begin." John
started. "Since it is the largest part
of the situation I find myself in."

John hesitated.

"It's called God Spelling. I learned
to do it before I was aware I was doing
it. I cast it first on salt crystals so
that when combined with one specific
other element a bond would be created
making a solid, unbreakable material. I
then used that material to base all of
my other God Spells on. From it I

created watchers, glow bugs, cleaners,
and all of White City in its entirety.
I built it completely over the ocean
because I couldn't afford to buy land.
So I made it, my city over water. All
of it made primarily out of salt."

"Why?" Harvey asked.

"It all seemed to be out of
necessity at the time" John returned.
"I don't think you have time for all of
the details. I'll just let you know
that they were all made for the love of
another. The first God Spell, on salt
itself, was out of love for your
father, my son."

"And the others?" Harvey asked.

"Watchers were out of jealousy over
my husband, Tomm's, indiscretions."

Harvey had never heard of Tomm
before.

"And the glow bugs?" Harvey
continued.

"There was a time when Tomm was in a
great deal of danger, I made glow bugs
accidentally when I feared for his
life. They took on a life of their own
from there."

"Cleaners?"

"They were really builders. I
designed White City, and then
programmed it into those little crab
like machines I had made. When the God
Spell took, they built the place. It
was virtually empty for a very long

time. Anthony, Tomm and myself lived there alone until Anthony decided he needed a few women around."

"My father had more than a few women around." Harvey stated.

"I know, he got that from his mother, at least he didn't have any weird ethical and moral hang-ups. Sue's family was obsessive to the point of psychosis."

"I hate to tell you this." Harvey said. "But your story sounds quite delusional to me. Are you sure you don't have a few? …"

"Don't be naïve Harvey. Think it through. I am 136 years old. Do you think that's normal?"

"You have a point." Harvey was still understandably suspicious. "Would you care to demonstrate your power?" Harvey tempted.

"If it was that simple do you really think I would have come collapsing into your arms?" John was obviously antagonized by the question.

"I'm sorry." Harvey explained. "But your story is just a little difficult to believe. If I hadn't seen you before and didn't know just a little bit about your past I don't think I would have even hung around to listen to it."

"Do you still want to hear the rest?" John asked.

"There's more?"

"Oh yes. There is a lot more. Somewhere in the mix you'll find out where your mother's gone to."

"You know where my mother is then?"

"No, not at the moment. Nor will I be looking for her. That woman is dangerous."

"My mother is dangerous?"

"You saw her hit me didn't you?"

Harvey thought about it for a moment. "There is something your keeping from me." He accused.

Perhaps it was true in a way. Mars was trying to hide Harvey from his mother though. Not the other way around.

"I think that what I've told you needs to sink in before I tell you the rest." John said pulling on his boots. "For now, let's go shopping. We will need some supplies for the trip."

Why would I want to go anywhere with you?" Harvey was suddenly feeling very stubborn.

"I thought you wanted proof that my story was true." John said.

"I do, but how will a trip solve anything?"

"Seeing is believing. I need to get to my lab. I'll show you everything when we get there. Then there is your mother. If you don't come you won't hear her story and may never find her." John said as he stood. Harvey followed suit. "There is also this." John said as he leaned in and gave Harvey a fierce, strong kiss. The kind of kiss only a man can give another man.

Harvey melted. He had wanted that kiss. He wrapped his arms around John and tugged him close. Locked together he forgot at once the wrongs and betrayals of past friends and lovers. He would go.

The result of the failed God Spell on salt was tumultuous. Nothing worked anymore. Windows simply vanished out of all sorts of things. Gears inside of transmissions and machines disappeared. It seemed that there was one part made from salt in every modern device that was in use.

"That's why the city got so quiet." Harvey thought out loud as he and John headed out to buy new cloths. They walked for miles in the cold. Harvey was freezing when they got to their destination.

"What was that you were saying?" John asked.

"Well there are no cars out." Harvey stated the obvious.

"I told you a little about it in the room. My God Spells are ruined. Now the world must live without them."

"Why do you call them God Spells?" Harvey asked sarcastically. "Are you a God?"

"Yes." John said. "As a matter of fact I am Mars."

Harvey snorted a disbelieving laugh.

"If you don't mind I'd rather explain the terms and conditions latter when you have a clearer mind."

Their destination was a sporting goods store. Harvey began to worry. They entered. John grabbed a cart and began loading the thing up. It filled quickly with backpacks, cold weather clothing, coats, hiking shoes and hats.

"Don't you at least want my shoe size before you buy me shoes?" Harvey couldn't help but ask.

"I know your foot size Harvey. I've known it from the moment you walked into White City."

Harvey stared at the man in disbelief. *"Who was this man, this creature he was with?"* He thought.

True evil doesn't go away just because it has been forced to hide its face. Terrorists, anarchists, even just run of the mill criminally minded people had spent their lives unable to act on their unnatural needs to rise in the world, standing on the backs of the pure and the innocent. Within the muddy back current of a soul touched by evil there was a knowledge that the glow bugs wouldn't be there forever. These people still thought dark thoughts that were never acted on, wishing for and hoping for misery on others. Their day would come again. They tested their limits only tentatively at first.

Kimmy, who had been Bobby's girlfriend for as long as either of them could remember, hated it when he disagreed with her. The next time he disagreed she grabbed his hair and pulled it until he said yes to whatever she wanted. She laughed at him.

He was looking at her with teary-eyed dismay, hurt not by the little violence done him but by the question. *"Why would someone want to hurt me?"* It was only a matter of time before more evil would come, especially since there were now food and shelter shortages, no transportation, and no police to keep the order.

In the aftermath created by the loss of such a huge protective force, natural defenses had weakened. Violence would be set loose like a marble that rested in a sling shot without tension for a time, until the glow bugs like a big fist pulled it taught, then with their disappearance released the marble.

Mars knew it was coming. It was this that moved him to get Harvey out of Chicago quickly. He could handle a few small encounters, but he doubted he was in any condition to handle a mob.

Harvey seemed to be following Mars not
out of honesty, but more as if Mars
were a funny little mystery. Mars saw
Harvey's innocence clearly. The entire
human race was ripe with it. The
seriousness of life had been somewhat
removed with the removal of violence.
For a century the world had become an
ongoing cocktail party. Living in this
altered reality had left the world
primed for victimization. Mars thought
of the aftermath that would come like a
sort of hangover on the mind of the
combined human consciousness after a
season of heavy drinking.

　　"You really think I'm going to go on
this cross country race of madness
don't you?" Harvey said looking at the
heavy packs.

　　"For now I'll settle with a hotel at
the edge of town, away from the busy
city." Mars said. He knew that it would
be as far as they could go that day,
the edge of town, and that by morning
much would have changed. The real
trouble would have begun.

*Harvey dreamed a very strange dream.
He didn't dream that he had everything
he needed. Nor did he dream that he had
everything he wanted, but rather that
he got whatever he craved. Although
there was no question that Harvey was a
man, and quite human, there was a part*

of him that was nebulous and moved of it's own accord. He found himself confronted with a strange question. What and who was he? It should be a simple question, but really isn't easy to answer. What a man is; isn't formed in his thoughts, not even in his actions, although actions are a warped reflection of a man's soul. The soul isn't the man though. Harvey found that the only way to know a man was to see what he craved. To see this, certain questions had to be asked.

If you had power, real power, not just to have what you needed, because if you dig deep you would discover that your needs have been covered from the day you were born. Otherwise you would already be dead. That power will always be yours until you move to the next world and the next life. Nor to precipitate into reality what you create with the thoughts in your head. You would soon find such things hollow and meaningless.

If, however, you had a power that gave you what you craved, what would the result be? You would not stay what you are.

Would you fly away as an immortal canary? Would you become the living wind, blowing where you would? How long would the real you crave human existence? Would you be the picture of

perfection, someone so beautiful you
could fuck anyone you wanted? Would you
become fire incarnate and burn away
everything you fear and hate?
   Who are you really?
   Harvey's mind fuck echoed. His heart
beat heavy and he turned in his sleep
to pull the man next to him close as if
that could keep him what he was now and
keep his real self from emerging. His
hands found the soft trail of silver
hair that ran from chest in a line down
to that sculpted flesh that defines
ultimate masculinity. Thick, hard,
rigid, unforgiving, penetrating
straight to the core of things and at
the same time beautiful, pale, white
and pink, so soft to the touch, every
thumping thrust being just the kind of
rape everyone needs and wants because
it means we can't ask the question that
would get the answer to the question
that haunts us the most. "Who are we?"

   Morning was cold and Harvey woke
with his arms wrapped tightly around
John. John was still sleeping.
   They had found the hotel in a state
of exhaustion. Well, Harvey had been
exhausted. John was made of stronger
metal. Harvey had never needed to walk
so far before with all of the easy
modes of transportation available. Now

that they were gone walking seemed to be the only way to get around.

Harvey's legs were stiff. So was his dick. Right now it was resting comfortably between John's butt cheeks, throbbing lightly. John stirred a little as Harvey gave a little thrust for adjust then buried his face into the back of John's neck.

"Can we talk?" Harvey asked.

"I thought you'd never ask." John said. "What would you like to talk about?"

"Well if you are a God why can't we just, you know, disappear and then reappear in your lab?"

Mars was a little startled by the question. Not because of the traveling bit but because he had once again underestimated Harvey and his ability to cut through the bullshit and get to the meat of the situation. John would have to tell all to answer the question.

"Let's start at the café shall we." John said.

"The one we just left a few days ago?" Harvey rolled onto his back and gave a good tug on his erection. It felt good but he wished John were doing it for him.

"The same." John rolled over so he could look Harvey over then settled on his side leaning against Harvey. His rather large tool lying over Harvey's leg, the end of it nudging against Harvey's balls.

Harvey groaned a bit. He thought he would pop if this teasing continued.

"The reason I was exhausted was because I had just had a confrontation with two other Gods. One of them was your mother."

Harvey's erection turned immediately flaccid and he felt very sober. "My mother is a Goddess?"

"Your mother is The Goddess, you know, *mother earth?*"

"Oh my God."

"That would be me." John whispered into Harvey's ear. It tickled and Harvey liked it.

"Anyway," John said, "Gods can tell when one of the other Gods are moving around in the way you just described, and I don't want to be found by her and that eagle, Jupiter, until I can defend myself. They damn near killed me the last time."

"My mother tried to kill you?" Harvey felt stunned. "Why?"

"Your mother and her lackey Jupiter both tried to kill me. Harvey, understand this. The intelligence that possessed your mother and made her into a Goddess doesn't share mind space with the people whose bodies she needs. It's

not really your mother doing these
things."

It struck like a hangover. Gia was
sick. She had forgotten some of the
more important rules about God Spells,
and was remembering why so few Gods had
the stamina to maintain life on the
surface of their worlds.

Although the men on the planet had
long ago disconnected themselves from
her long reach, every woman had
maintained just a little bit of a
connection. She hadn't considered the
people on the planet hers, but they
still claimed her. Now they were full
of panic and chaos. The people were
desperate for food, and violence had
once again been set loose upon the
world.

*"How could I have even considered
wiping them all out?"* Gia thought.

Gia had long ago placed a God Spell
upon the early primate males to her
liking. It had been only a nudge. From
that they had grown on their own into
the civilization that existed now. Her
spell hadn't produced what she needed
though, so she had placed a God Spell
on the females of the species.

The females were symbiotic and
needed the males to perpetuate the
race, but it had worked. Gia's God
Spell had finally produced what she

needed. She had many new hosts to live within.

She'd made it a habit to use primarily the women as hosts because there was something strange within the men's genetic structure that hindered the flow of her power.

Over time a net of life developed from that first God Spell she had laid on men. The net kept her fed and full of energy. It was an unplanned bonus. She received just a little life force from each living woman. Now with them all sick with hunger she was finding herself starved and when the world panic brought with it death Gia would grow even sicker.

Jupiter cawed upon her shoulder.

"Yes I have acted rashly. I slept too long this time, but you have to admit that Mars has a dark past. I just couldn't trust what he was up to. Still I should have taken more time to study it. It's too late though. His God Spells are crushed, and I had no idea that they were so beneficial to me."

Jupiter raised the feathers on his wing and nibbled the end of one.

The irony in Gia's situation was that she needed the God they had just crushed or she would be forced to slumber once again while she sought out a new host. Her current host would die.

Trista who was still locked inside
knew this as well. Inside her womb
where she remained to this day
connected to Harvey she sent him a
message.

Chapter Sixteen

Past and Present

Don't Touch It. It's Mine.

Sue was infuriated. Do you know what happens when a newly seated world ruler gets pissed off? Not only had she been embarrassingly soaked to the core but she had also lost both of the prisoners she most prized. True one of them had been ordered to the execution block but he had been hers and now he was gone. He had slipped away from her. Now there was only one thing she could think of that might settle her nerves.

"Chaz?"

"Yes Madam President?"

"Send my son in from wherever he is please."

"Yes Madam President…"

Sue waited a few minutes after Chaz had left the room before she headed to the closet for some fresh clothing. It was just as she had expected. The clothing she had in her closet wasn't even suited for the nasty whores working the street corners.

She looked into the mirror at her frizzed out hair and washed her makeup streaked face. After combing her hair down she looked very plain. It was at that moment that Anthony entered.

"Anthony?"

"Yes Ma'am."

"Anthony, I've told you to call me mom. I know I wasn't there for you when you were growing up but I am your mother. Besides, you are royal heir to the world throne. How would it look if you didn't call me mom?"

"Yes mother." Anthony said, still making it sound terribly formal. It was enough for Sue.

"I want to spend some much needed mother son time with you."

"Mother son time?" Anthony asked a little mocking.

"Anthony, don't be rude. I found your father you know. I asked him if he wanted to see you and he left in quite a big hurry. I guess he didn't want to be bothered."

Anthony stifled a tear. He didn't believe her, but he missed his father.

"You'll go with me won't you?" Sue manipulated. "I just want to go shopping and have a facial, maybe get my hair done."

"Well…" Anthony stammered.

"Wonderful, I'll call an escort service for us." Sue rang a bell. "You

are such a good boy." Sue cajoled not
even aware of how condescending it
sounded. Not caring that Anthony would
much rather play video games in his
huge and over decorated private prison.
At least they took his mind off of his
kidnapping.

The escorts arrived. Sue clapped
like a happy schoolgirl and off they
all went to go shopping.

"Have someone clear the mall of all
of the rabble before we get there. I
want the place empty except for a
cashier at each door, only one, and put
a guard on each one. I don't want any
mistakes or it will be your ass." Sue
leaned in and whispered to Chaz as they
left her private quarters. "And make an
appointment with my salon for me."

Shopping always cleared Sue's mind.
She had a lot of things to do and she
needed to move on with them. After all,
there were reasons she had gone to all
the trouble of creating a world
government. There were changes to be
made and she felt that she should be
the one to make them. The world had
always wanted a God to worship, and
they had always wanted one who would
step in and punish the wicked. Sue had
decided to become that figure.

She hummed to herself as she picked
out a blouse and handed it to the clerk
standing next to her.

Anthony was milling around
aimlessly.

After a few minutes of choosing what
to try on Sue made her way to a fitting
room.

This was her favorite part of
shopping. She tried on the first
outfit, a stunning evening gown. It fit
her figure perfectly, accentuating just
the right places. She smiled at herself
in the mirror then stepped out to show
it off.

"What do you think Anthony?" Sue
chirped at her boy.

"Nice." Anthony said sounding bored.

Sue sighed and stepped back into the
fitting room. She took it off and
tossed it aside. She had hoped Anthony
would warm up to her this afternoon. So
far all he had done was drag her
already bad mood down another notch.
She put on her clothes and left the
fitting room.

"Put it in a box and charge it to my
account." She told the clerk. "Have it
delivered."

Maybe the makeover would help since
shopping wasn't.

Anthony couldn't help being annoyed
with his mother. He'd seen the letter

she'd left to his father years ago when
she had gone. Anthony had found it in a
box in the attic. Now she made it sound
as if she had been chased away and that
his life with his dad's was some
horrible torture he should never have
experienced.

His life with his dad's had been
really wonderful until she had shown
up. Then Tomm had gone away. The years
after that were torture. He had loved
Tomm, and all he had ever heard was how
horrible the man was for abandoning his
husband and boy. Anthony had cried
almost constantly over it. His dad John
had been so lost that he spent all of
his time in his lab. Anthony had lost
it all over night and the one person
who had marked the end of his happiness
was right here with him, his mother,
Sue. He couldn't stand her, and he was
sure she had something to do with
Tomm's disappearance. He knew she was
capable of anything. She had kidnapped
him. He was locked up and guarded
constantly. She was ruthless.

Still even through the annoyance of
having to be with her on this rediculas
charade, the bad feelings weren't
enough for him not to be distracted by
the gorgeous woman who was doing his
mother's nails. He had been left in the
company of all male guards for a very
long time now, and had no access to any

semblance of woman other than his mother. Her territorial nature generally removed all presence of other females from her vicinity. Due to this stifling environment, and the fact that his mother was not even remotely attractive to Anthony, along with other very strong natural under currents, Anthony was unable to not stare. He could feel the blood moving around in his drawers. He knew what was going on in his pants. He wanted to find a private place to himself and just imagine the girl naked while he touched himself. He was so uncomfortable he thought he was going to die from want, and was it just him or was she eyeing him over. Anthony grabbed a magazine and opened it over his lap. He knew it was an obvious cover up, but he needed to do something.

"Your nails are done Ma'am. Jackie is going to do your massage and facial. She's in back."

"Excellent." Sue chirped, and she got up and hurried toward the room where the facial mask would be applied. Halfway through the door she stopped and looked back to Anthony. "Will you be alright?" She asked.

"Fine." Anthony said not looking up.

Sue shook her head in frustration. *"The boy was in need of some domestic skills, maybe a tutor."* She thought.

Jill had been noticing the young
man. *"Jr. Mrs. President."* She thought.
She had seen the way he was looking at
her. She did think he was attractive.
By the look of the bulge he was
carrying in his pants, he was ready to
go. Her husband had been pretty
inattentive lately, and she liked being
looked at. Now that his mother was out
of the way she could look him over. He
was quite a catch, good looking, well
mannered, well groomed, well endowed,
and from a very wealthy line. She could
do worse. She'd done worse.

Right now he was pretending not to
notice her. His face was buried in a
beauty magazine, but she could tell he
was really watching her from the corner
of his eye. From where she was she made
busy cleaning up her station being
careful to walk and move in just such a
way as to look enticing. She knew she
was treading on thin ice messing with
Sue's boy, but there was something
about him that made her feel aroused,
even drawn toward the idea of sex with
him.

Anthony noticed. He was watching her
pose. He was sure she was posing for
his benefit. Now with his mother
preoccupied he was free to notice
without her coming unglued. He looked
up from the magazine and now the full

force of his drive was surfacing. His
dick was pulling so tight on his pants
that it was threatening to tear through
the zipper just to get at the girl. She
looked to it and it was obvious that
she wanted it. Still he made no move.
He was inexperienced.

"What if I'm wrong?" He thought. He
didn't think he could handle the
humiliation of such a thing. He looked
back down at the magazine and planned
to let the mood slide by. He could take
matters in hand when he got back to his
room, although he hated to do it there.
He knew that the guards posted to check
the cameras there watched everything.
He was sure they enjoyed watching him.
It made him nervous.

"So tell me Anthony." Jill said as
she swept across the room toward him,
making her move. "What kind of girls do
you like?" She continued casually
reaching down and taking the magazine
out of his hands. She smiled seeing
that he was ready to go underneath his
pants. She liked big. It made her feel
full, *"That's how I like my pussy.
Full!"* she thought.

Anthony began to tremble with
anticipation. Jill sat down next to him
and put her hand on his leg, high up
squeezing slightly, making Anthony jump
then go rigid all over.

"Do you think I'm pretty?" Jill
asked.

"Very." Anthony said. "Very pretty."
His voice cracked with tension. He
couldn't believe this was happening. Of
course he had fantasized, but he never
thought… He couldn't even move.

Jill lifted her hand from his leg
and took Anthony's wrist, pulling it
over to her own leg and slid his hand
up her smooth leg under her skirt.

Anthony was shaking like crazy as
his hand touched her there. She wasn't
wearing panties. His fingers slid over
everything. It was moist, soft and
slick. His fingers found every tiny
curve there and one or two fingers, for
a moment, found a place where they
slipped in.

Jill groaned as she let him fondle
her. It had been a long time. It had
been a long time since she had seen a
dick too. While he stroked and explored
her she was undoing his pants.

His dick sprung straight out as soon
as his zipper went down. It was long
and thick, and she slipped her hand in
gently to draw out the two rather big
heavy nuts that nestled close
underneath it. They too were large. It
appeared Anthony was quite well
endowed.

"*Good genetics.*" Jill thought. She
re maneuvered herself, even though it

forced his hand away from her pussy and repositioned herself so she could suck his dick. She brought it close to her lips licking it once across the head before she plunged down onto it forcing it down her throat even though it was a little uncomfortable for her to accommodate something so large. Still she wanted him to be impressed so she made sure that her chin pressed firmly against his balls so that every inch of him was in her mouth.

Anthony groaned. He never would have thought... *Damn! I'm already too close to cumming."* He thought. He reached down and pulled her away.

"Not so fast." He whispered. "It's been a long time for me."

"Me too." Jill whispered wiping her chin as she went in for a kiss.

The kisses were hot and desperate. Jill hiked up her skirt not caring about his warning and while she kissed him she pressed his still wet dick into herself. His arms went instinctively around her, and she began her slow rhythmic motion.

Jill was already cumming. She had never had problems in that area, so a quickie was good for her. She was groaning as she picked up the pace and soon she knew he was cumming too. He pulled her to him tightly just as the door opened.

"Anthony! What are you? ..." Sue was
taking in the scene. "Jill?" Sue's
relaxation shot away replaced by a
tight-lipped fury. "How dare you!"

Sue was across the room before
either Jill or Anthony could move or
respond to her entrance. She grabbed
Jill by the hair and flung her across
the room then was on top of her
slapping her face hard and fast.

Anthony moved instinctively and ran
to her defense while tucking his penis
back into his trousers. He grabbed
Sue's arm before she could land another
blow, but in doing so he found himself
the target.

Before she could stop herself Sue
had slapped him as hard as she could
across the face.

He was stunned. You see even though
Anthony knew deep down that he was
kidnapped and that Sue was not a nice
woman, he had held a fantasy about her
locked inside, that some day he would
be able to call her mom and feel it. He
had loved his fathers and would never
trade either of them away, but he knew
his mother had been out there, and he
had always wanted her to come, to be in
his life.

Sue stopped in her tracks and looked
at the welts on Anthony's face. "Let's
go!" She said as she turned and stormed
out of her former favorite salon.

Sue hadn't seen it but she had broken the fantasy Anthony had harbored about her. He knew now that he was just a prisoner, and that she didn't care. The sting of the slap had been more than physical. It had severed the potential bond between mother and son.

Anthony took long enough to pick Jill up from the floor.

"I'm sorry." He whispered to a sobbing girl. "I have to go." He gently let her go not knowing that she would conceive and that she would bear his first child under another man's name. In his head something happened and from that moment on he never could stay with a woman after he had came inside her. It just wasn't safe for them to be with him. The rest of his life he would just cum then leave.

"It's time." Sue thought as they were on their way home in the limousine. *"I will start with that little slut Jill. It'll teach her to touch what is mine."*

Chapter Seventeen

In the Future

Dream, Dream, Dream

Harvey felt a little queasy this
morning. He wasn't sure why. For days
he had been worried about his mother,
and now he couldn't get her out of his
mind.

John and Harvey had been traveling
for weeks now, and Harvey was
exhausted. John was relentless in his
pace and seemed tireless. At the end of
each day Harvey climbed, naked, into a
sleeping back with the man, God, and
slept waking up to an intense sexual
appetite that was always satiated by
John who really knew how to handle
things. Yet still he was worn out. John
seemed not to notice though and they
kept their steady speed of travel.

They had begun to avoid the roads
and highways now. Since there was
little food in the towns and cities
people had become desperate. It was no
longer safe to encounter anyone. The
world was in a state worse than
depression.

The loss of the God Spell had caused
holocaust. Many had died, and more were
dieing. Harvey felt terrible for those
who they had come across who were sick
and starving, but he soon discovered
that they were hostile when they
discovered that they were hungry and he
had been fed well. They perceived him
as not a healthy fed man, but as a man
who was withholding food from them. He
was in their eyes a murderer for not
sharing with all until he like them was
starving.

John appeared to have already
learned this lesson and carefully
steered them both safely away from all
of these uncomfortable situations.

At first Harvey had been angry that
John didn't use his God power to help
these people.

"What good is your power if it isn't
used?" Harvey demanded one day.

"Do you think my power is
limitless?" John said. "Don't you know
that were I to just wave my hand and
feed the whole world it would kill me
and the world would only be fed for a
day while I was forced to slumber?"
John frowned at Harvey and Harvey felt
scorned.

"I am going to help them Harvey."
John said as his voice softened. "That
is why we are traveling now. That is
why we journey south. I will go to my

lab and there I will be strong enough
to help, but getting there might kill
me."

"I don't understand." Harvey said.
"How could this trip kill you?"

"I'm getting tired Harvey." John
said.

"I'm fucking exhausted Harvey said.
Let's take a day to rest then." Harvey
suggested. "Besides you seem to be
tireless to me."

"It's your exhaustion that is
killing me Harvey and I don't
understand why you are staying so
tired. I have been pouring my God Spell
into you every night while we sleep and
every morning while we make love,
trying to keep you alive, but still you
are exhausted. Every day it is harder
for me to recharge you. If we stop for
a day it may make us one day too late
and I have much to show you. If I die
too soon then you will be in the dark.
We still have a month of travel and
that is a long way."

"If I'm such a burden then why have
you brought me with you?" Harvey asked
feeling a little angry that he was
being accused of dragging John down.

"Harvey, You will know how important
you are to me soon enough. I need you
and you alone can fit the purpose you
were born for." John looked into
Harvey's dark eyes searching for a way

around the conversation, looking for
the source of the guilt and anger.
"Don't worry about it so much Harvey.
Maybe I'll find out what is using so
much of my life force in you. Then
there will be less a burden. I need you
alive, and something is draining you.
That something is a new attachment and
I will discover it's source and remedy
the drain if possible. It will take
time though."

"Do you think it is Gia?" Harvey
asked. "Would she try to kill me?"

"I thought it was at first, but it
is not a God that is draining your life
energy. I think it is a part of
yourself, a part that is strange to my
mind and remains hidden from me."

"Hidden?" Harvey questioned.

"Don't worry on it Harvey, lets just
keep moving."

Twenty minutes later Harvey was
following behind John, keeping pace,
but stumbling. He was incredibly tired.
He had hoped that John had helped him
out by telling him about the strange
drain that he was experiencing, and
that it was not physical in nature. It
made sense to Harvey because he wasn't
sick. He was so tired though.

As they walked Harvey thought on it
thinking about what John had said. That
it was something within himself, a part

of him. Maybe he could find it and tell
John so that it could be remedied.

Harvey found himself concentrating
on the problem. He was searching his
soul for a parasite. For a part of him
that was eating away his life.

After a while he found himself
falling into a trance, a strange
meditation. The world around him,
although crisp to the eyes became
unfocused and unnoticed as Harvey began
to sink into his own consciousness. He
recognized the feeling. It wasn't
dissimilar to the effects of his
favorite drug of the past. Harvey had
spent years lost in such a muddled
dream state and somehow had survived
it. Yet there was no green haze
floating around him here. The world
wasn't becoming some strange silent
film. It was just slipping away, or
maybe he was slipping away from it.

Harvey found that he was falling
into himself. The memories of a hundred
days of crumbling civilization flooded
through him. Within those memories he
discovered wounds that he hadn't even
known existed. None had healed. All
bled freely. The reason he hadn't
notice them was because he had been
numb to everything.

Somewhere deep within his mind
sanity hummed it's soft tune, but he
was to far away from that place and was

being tossed in the whirlwind of his
broken world.

He remembered words spoken by a wise
old man. Someone from another time,
another place, someone he trusted. He'd
been told that his doom was coming for
him, a force that was wearing him down,
an unknown force. Something that even a
God incarnate couldn't stop was
destroying him.

Harvey couldn't see himself. Had he
been able to he would have seen where
he had fainted while walking.

Mars sat, legs crossed, with
Harvey's head resting in his lap. The
God's hands pressed against Harvey's
temples, concentrating on the consuming
task of keeping Harvey from slipping
away into oblivion. Such was his
importance to the God. A value Harvey
didn't recognize couldn't understand or
see.

Harvey was drenched with sweat, on
the edge of death, all of his strength
spent holding that force threatening
him at bay.

Harvey dreamed. Inside he was full
of color. He walked in familiar
surroundings. He was in his city, his
New Orleans. It was green and the air
was moist. The heat was unbearable yet
so delicious. It was early evening and
the city would cool soon. The lightning

bugs would blink on and off over the lawns of a thousand homes.

Harvey was so young. His life was new and today had been the first time he had been made love to by a man. His glow bug shown brilliantly with the color of his newly awakened self. He was so happy to finally find what direction his life might take in the world.

Harvey's friends had matured so much faster than he had. Most of them were the kind of men who would make babies. They were lovers of women. Their glow bugs changing to a brilliant blue telling the world that they wanted women. The whole time Harvey's glow bug remained white marking him off limits for sexual advancements from others. Until his bug turned color he was innocent and any advances would be recognized as an act of violence. Violence meant pain. No one wanted that kind of pain.

Harvey was on his way home. He was so proud of his newly found sexual maturity and he was exited to share the experience with his mother, Trista. He knew she would be excited with his coming of age. It would remind her of her own coming of age.

Walking from the city to Harvey's home would take a very long time. Their little abode was outside of the dikes

and rested on top of a small high knoll
in the middle of a swamp. It had
belonged to his family before slavery
had been abolished in the old U.S.A.

The house was made of mud, stick and
stone. The windows were open to the air
and bore only screen and shutter to
hold back the storms. His friends
thought it a strange place. Harvey knew
it's secrets though and so he
understood its uniqueness.

The fact was that all of the women
in his family had been witches. His
mother was one. It was an undeniable
fact. His family line also bore only
daughters.

Harvey was an anomaly. His mother
said that his father's spirit had been
rare and powerful and so she had bore a
son.

His mother's glow bug was lavender.
This marked her as a lover of both
women and men. She said it was the
witch's way. Harvey had assumed that
all his grandmothers had been like that
also, even back when such things were
secret and not spoken about. He had
heard stories of a time when a person
could expect violence upon them or even
death were their sexual affairs
discovered.

It was no secret between them that
Trista had hoped for many grandbabies
from Harvey. She would miss the dream

of it, but she would also know what it would mean. She could teach him the art of witchcraft.

The hover bike made good time over the swampland. Harvey had set it to auto pilot so that he could just look at the scenery. The water lilies were in full bloom and the cypress swayed gently in the breeze. Home was just around the bend.

The hover bike set down to park mode just a little way from the house. The flowers up the walk were dazzling.

He started his walk to the front door. His mother opened the door before he even came close to reaching it. The smell of fresh stew hit Harvey making his stomach growl. Charms and wind chimes made from all manner of bones or earthy things rattled and rang in the breeze. Many of them had been hung in the trees around the house generations ago. They would stay where they were for generations to come.

"Come eat you some supper." Trista offered with her thick accent. She was a beautiful woman despite the scars she bore from adolescent acne. Her yellow eyes glimmered in the evening sunset.

"Thank you momma." Harvey said. He had to duck to gain entrance to the house but once inside he had more than enough room to stand.

There was only one room in this
dwelling. It served all purposes with
the exception of the toilet. His mother
told him years ago that it was the way
of all witches. The kitchen is where
the fire is kept. It is therefore where
all elements are brought together,
earth, air, fire and water.

The toilet was in the wild because
we partake of the earth to exist here
and to the earth all things must be
returned. It was a polluted mind who
thought it would be a good idea to pile
all the shit together in one place to
spoil the land and draw flies.

Trista scooped the big wooden dipper
into the kettle and poured stew into
Harvey's bowl. Harvey didn't ask what
was in it. It would taste good
regardless of what it was. She was an
excellent cook.

"Harvey! Your glow bug has turned."
Harvey smiled as she noticed.

...

Something didn't seem right. Why
were his mother's eyes green?

...

"Don't let me die!" Trista lunged in
at him and yelled in his face. Somehow
she never moved toward him though.

...

"*She should be telling me about the
blood test results. Why isn't she
telling me about the father I didn't*

know I even had? Today was the day we decided to move to White City." Harvey thought.

...

"I'm dying Harvey. Gia is slipping into slumber. You must save me!"

"Mom?"

"Hurry Harvey. Make a move."

"I don't know how to save you. What should I do?" Harvey said. The cottage was fading away into a white mist.

"Use witchcraft Harvey."

"You never taught me how. I don't know any spells."

"You'll have to do it the hard way. The magic is inside you. It always was. The spells are just a way of telling it what to do. Find the magic and tell it what you want it to do." Trista's voice carried off into the distance.

The house and the swamp were quickly fading away.

Harvey didn't know what to do. He needed magic. He bent his mind around the idea. Focused all of his weight on the want of it. He missed his mother. He wanted her back. He needed her.

"The magic is inside you." The whisper of his mother's voice echoed.

"Inside me." He thought.

He was already inside. He was unconscious and dreaming. He knew it now. Still there was urgency to this dream that drove him to search his soul for an answer. He looked at every aspect of self he could think of, trying to find some invisible power he needed.

What he discovered was his frustration, and an anger that held a fire he had never tasted. He found his emotion. His love for a man he barely knew. He found the stormy sea of sexual pleasure he had dove into so many times.

His magic was inside his emotion. He had been numb and apathetic for so many years, but his greatest power was in his ability to feel. He let all of the feelings he had held pent up for so long out, all the loss of his friends and loved ones drowned in the calamity that befell White City.

If he had been able to move his body he would have been a knot of tension. His body was limp and unmoving though.

He dove through the fog around him. Forcing the house in the swamp to return. His mother was in the doorway smiling at him.

"Harvey, you came to me."

"Mom, what do I do? How do I save you?"

"Come with me and look at what has become of us."

He followed his mother inside there on the floor lay a body. It was his mom.

"She has complete control of it, and she sleeps. I am cast out, and my strength will fade until I become mist."

"What will save you?"

"I need a body, just like the Gods need one. I need a host. You must find one for me."

"Won't it kill the person there though?"

"It's me or them." She said. "Don't you want me to live?"

"Yes but…"

Harvey was crying. He couldn't loose his mother, but he wouldn't kill for her. There had to be another answer. He began to let go of the swamp and his mother.

"Harvey? Harvey, come back, please…"

Harvey looked into his magic for an answer. Instinctually he knew that there was another way. His emotions burned like hot flame, but they smelled like the woods and the life around him. Inside himself he was awakened to something new. He could feel the cosmos turning on its axis like a little science toy he had wound up and set on the counter as a child. The world around him was sparks of tiny light that spun in their own turnings. The micro cosmos vs. the macro cosmos, all was a connected pattern. Then the answer spun into his mind. He saw them

nestled together within the trees and
knew they were alone and doomed to die
without their mother.

They were smart and not too far from
where he was laying. He could see
himself with his head in Mars's lap. He
could feel the ocean close by. He
hadn't realized they were so close to
where White City once soared over the
water.

He could for a moment see the
dreaming of the universe. There were
infinite overlapping dreams each one
wishing for the physical material that
would make it real.

Harvey sank his magic into it all
and watched the pattern of the universe
rearrange itself to fit his idea. As
each tiny spark redirected itself it
touched a billion others that
redirected their path, then like a
ripple on the surface of a pond his
spell was cast in fire and water.

Harvey opened his eyes. He was
tired, but he had undone the mystery
that was killing him. He would live,
and so would his mother.

Chapter Eighteen

Past and Present

Freedom and Liberty for All

For years Sue had made plans. In fact she had made plans within plans. Not only was she prepared for what she was going to do here within this little city she called home but she was now in position for a global strike.

The little sexual episode that she had witnessed between her son and that bitch down town only confirmed that she was needed, and that her plans were the right thing to do. Her children needed to be taken care of, and she was going to take care of them. They needed a firm hand and punishment. Then they would all be taught the right way to behave. It was time to put the list in effect. First she needed to add a name to the list though. That name needed to be right up at the top. Jill was an adulteress. She was stepping out on her husband, in doing so had corrupted Sue's own little boy Anthony. She would be the first to get the arrest.

"Chaz?" Sue called out. There was no response.

"Chaz?" She said a bit more forcefully this time needing the attention of her messenger boy. Still there was no response. Realizing that he was not at his post Sue instead went and rang the little electric bell she'd had installed and waited for some one to come to her. She sat in her comfortable office chair and began typing Jill's name right up top in her black list of sexual deviants. She had them all listed.

For years she'd had her private army building prisons for this occasion. It was finally time to put them to use. There were millions of these large camps. All of them had been built under the guise of war shelters on restricted military zones. They were already fully staffed and ready to fill up. All of the staff members had gone through her personal training regime. All had been broken and brought to their knees and were qualified to be her personal guards. All had been completely successfully brainwashed, and those who she felt had been too difficult to brain wash had been disposed of. Now they would all praise her for their day of purpose was at hand.

The first thing Tomm did after his
escape was return to his home looking
for his lost family. He found nothing
there that was his. The home belonged
to others now. He was lost after that.
He went to the only place he felt was
really his. He went to the ocean. It
was like him at this moment.

Clouds stretched from horizon to
horizon and the cold wind stirred the
surface of the sea into a frenzy of
waves, all intent on washing the land
away, into the water.

Because it was cold Tomm was alone.
No one wanted to be cold and alone
here. The sound of the surf blotted out
all other noise leaving a sensation of
solitude. Solitude was exactly what he
had. It was all he'd had for years. He
had oceans of it.

The stench that precedes eminent
death floated in the air like a
disease. To Sue it was the sweet smell
of victory. She was bringing these
sinners justice. Every one of the
people in the camps had committed sins
before her. Every one was a cheater or
a liar, a thief or sexual deviant. Not
like her. She was perfectly flawless,
not a hair out of place. She was here
for one reason. To show her boy the
repercussions of sin before he became a
sinner. His soul was at stake.

Anthony curled his upper lip with the smell of the camp. He was appalled by the state of the prisoners. He wanted to cry. He wanted to help them but with Sue so close by he had to keep a straight face. A hard face meant she would not add him to the list of her victims. In her eyes it would mean that she had taught him the error of his ways.

It had been one month since his mother had shown the world the extent of her madness. She had so much power over her military though. Not a single one would be dissuaded from her command. She had spent decades obtaining the names of people she deemed to be criminals and sexual deviants. There were no trials. They had all been arrested.

She hadn't arrested a single drug addict or alcoholic though. She said that they were the product of a deranged society and she would cure them. The fact was that she had plans for them. Addicts, she had found, made very reliable soldiers. She needed soldiers. Drug addicts were very easy to brainwash. They would serve her well after she put them through her own personal training regime.

Anthony was so lost in the horror of his surroundings that he nearly ran into Sue when she stopped. She was

silent and Anthony looked her over
trying to gage what she had in mind.
She stood before him like a stone
monolith. Her face showed no emotion.
The corners of her mouth leaning ever
so slightly downward in the permanent
frown she had developed over the years
of her life spent in anger. She was
staring at one of the prisoners.

Anthony followed her gaze to the
woman lying in her own filth in a small
cell with not even a cot or toilette.
Once a month the place would be sprayed
out with a fire hose, but that hadn't
happened yet. He looked back at Sue.
What was she going to do?

"You see the product of your sin?"
She said to him.

"What?" he returned shaking his head
ever so slightly.

"Look closer." Sue said with a form
of cruelty he had never heard directed
at him before. He looked again.

He looked at the woman. Trying to
squint through the darkness.

"Perhaps some light then." Sue said.
The accompanying guard flipped the
switch and the cell lights came on.

She was facing the wall. Crouched in
the corner, hiding her face. Her
clothes, which had once been brightly
colored and expensive, were now filthy
and torn. She was bruised and terribly
thin. Her hair was cut nearly to her

skull with clippers. It had been a rough procedure. There were scabs to prove the brutality of it.

Anthony shook his head still not understanding.

"Still don't get it?" Sue asked.

"What do you want me to get?" Anthony asked. "She looks beaten and starved like everyone else here."

"Turn around!" Sue spat at the woman in the cell. The woman twitched violently when she was yelled at and began to shake uncontrollably.

"Turn around or be turned around by one of my guards!" Sue commanded.

Slowly the woman stood up and turned around looking down at the ground so low that her face was still hidden.

"Look at me!" Sue commanded.

The woman looked up, but not at Sue, She looked at Anthony. Those eyes. He knew those eyes.

"Jill?" Anthony said now recognizing her, remembering her in her salon, so beautiful, now so torn. He began to cry. "I'm so sorry Jill. I'm so very…"

"Enough!" Sue yelled. "We leave now!"

Anthony was shaking as they left the camp. He felt broken. He had done this to her. It was his fault she was here. If he hadn't touched her she would have never been on his mothers shit list. He felt guilty. It was exactly what his

mother had intended. The shame was
beginning to take form.

"Your prisoners are over fed." Sue
said to the captain of the guard on her
way out. "The one named Jill looks a
little bit fat."

"I'll see to it that they are given
less." The guard saluted.

"See to it then." Sue said.

Anthony's guilt and shame suddenly
turned to fury and anger. This woman
wasn't his mother. She was a monster.
It was never his fault that Jill came
to any of this. It was all Sue. She was
the embodiment of madness. She had
tortured and killed countless people
for her own selfish beliefs. Yet he did
feel guilty. He felt guilty because he
didn't know how to stop her.

Tomm had found an alley to sleep in.
It was dark and smelled of garbage
bins, but it was sheltered from the
autumn storms that had begun to creep
in off of the coast, and it had a
little spot in the back where he could
hide from the eyes of others. Since the
patrols had started he had taken to
hiding because the little glow bug drew
too much attention to him, and when met
with aggression it would always down
the soldiers in question.

He had found some level of peace
here although it was getting colder,

and he knew he couldn't stay here
forever. His coat wasn't that warm, and
would be less warm when things got wet.

It was nighttime, and he had been
sleeping when he was awakened by some
sounds. He lay still for a moment
listening.

*"Is it soldiers? Will I have to run
again?"* He thought. He remained quiet
and soon could hear and distinguish
what the sound was.

It had been a long time since he had
heard the sound of lovers. At first he
had thought the two men were wrestling,
but he could tell they were after
something different now. Tomm was
awakened to that arousal he'd once
known so well, his dick thickening and
lengthening on it's own just hearing
the sounds, the pittery pattery of men
masturbating in the dark.

Tomm reached into his pants and
massaged his stiffening dick. It was a
feeling he hadn't given in to for a
long time. It felt good. He knew that
getting caught would mean arrest and
prison camp for any of them. They no
doubt knew the same. It was in the
papers everywhere. Sue and her cure for
sin. He quietly unzipped his jeans and
pulled the big piece of meat out. It
was dark but he had looked at his own
dick enough times to know how thick it

was compared to other men. He wanted to
see the other men and their dicks.

He slipped from the shadows tugging
on his dick. The other two men came
into view instantly. The other men were
facing him and saw him just as quickly
as he saw them, both tugging on their
own dicks. In the moonlight he must
have looked beautiful. His hard muscled
arms and chest heaving and flexing in
rhythm to his hand motion. He could see
their white grins telling him they were
okay for a third party.

He stepped closer and one of the men
went to his knees running his tongue
over the end of Tomm's dick. Tomm
groaned quietly as the man took the
full length of it into his mouth. He
felt a little hypnotized by the
sensation, his hips thrusting lightly
and his balls swinging slightly to
thump into the man's chin. He hardly
noticed as the man stopped and turned
around. The gentleness of the man's
hair covered butt cheeks as he pressed
himself back into Tomm. His hole wet
and ready made the penetration soft and
easy. Tomm's dick slid slowly and
smoothly in.

The other man, the one getting his
dick sucked while Tomm was fucking the
cock sucker from the other end, kissed
Tomm lightly on the lips.

The man between them groaned, sucking on a dick while Tomm thrusted.

Tomm could feel each individual vein fill with every throbbing thrust and he savored the moment of climax as the tingling explosion started to make it's way from the little spot where his balls met his shaft down across the length of his dick toward the under side of his swollen dick head then exploded out the end and at the same time reverberating back up into him, hot and sweet. He shuddered with the thumping of his heart. He was alive again. He had been prisoner for such a long time and now he was alive again.

Tomm opened his eyes again and before him he watched his little glow bug lay to rest on the man's back, and there it split in two and became not one but two complete bugs. The other two men seemed not to notice this as they reached their own climax and the copulation was complete.

Not a word was spoken as they left the alley. They only nodded at one another in recognition of the temporary fulfillment of their forbidden desires.

Tomm stepped back into the shadow and watched them go. One of them with a new twinkling glow bug tagging along over his head just out of his vision.

Tomm fell back into the shadows tucking his dick back into his jeans.

He was so relaxed. It was getting cold.
He would travel south where the cold
wouldn't kill him in his homeless
state. He would look for someplace
remote where he could find escape from
Sue and her madness. He hoped there was
escape. At least he was allowed human
contact. His glow bug didn't deny him
that.

Mars was born again. John was still
there, but now was complete. He watched
Tomm through one of his viewers and
smiled. The glow bug was unexpected,
but it would serve him better than any
God Spell he could have thought up. God
Spells were like that. The best ones
were born instead of made.

What was once one glow bug were now
two. Two would become four until there
were thousands of them. Maybe millions.
Now Mars just needed to guide Tomm to
the place where he could do the most
good. He must guide the man toward
revolution. Sue would be stopped for
good. Peace would feel nice. The world
would bow to his will unaware.

Still Mars was a builder. He would
need something to occupy his time, and
He was still deeply in love with Tomm
and his son. They needed a home, and
Mars had always wanted to understand
the inner workings of this planet ruled
by Gia. She was still sleeping, and he

had time to explore without
repercussion. The smile on his face was
genuine. He hadn't felt so alive in
millennia, and his host had never felt
so alive. Together they were one to be
reckoned with.

"Follow Tomm my little toy." Mars
whispered to the little living machine.
"Show him what I'm up to. Guide him to
me and save the world."

The little screen immediately split
in two and grew into two complete crab
like viewer. The new screen showed a
clear picture of what it's counterpart
watched, an image of Mars and his
current surroundings.

"Move along then." Mars said. I have
work to do."

Mars then went about his plan. It
was going to hurt. He wasn't looking
forward to that part.

Sue was sitting in her office
smiling with pride. She had gotten
through to her son, and there was for
the moment nothing on her agenda. She
was basking in the joy of a job well
done just tapping her fingers on the
desk.

"Thunk! Thunk!" The knock on her
door brought her out of her calm.

"Yes?" She said. The door opened and
her new assistant entered. Chaz had
left her services. She was keeping a

close eye on him for possible trouble, but wasn't too concerned. He hadn't the stomach for richeousness.

"We have him." Her new assistant said. She still didn't know her new assistants name. It was better that way. He was from her personal guard and was loyal to a fault.

"Who?" She purred having received good news.

"Your ex-husband my lady."

Her smile broadened from ear to ear and she fell back into her chair.

"Send him to the camps. A little hunger will make him more amiable to my wishes."

"As you wish my lady." Her assistant responded.

"I have some work for you in an hour or two so stay handy."

"Yes my lady."

The door closed.

"*Just one loose end to tie up. I wonder how Tomm escaped and to where he has gone? All in time though.*" Sue thought. "*All in good time.*"

It wasn't long after Tomm got on the road to the south that he noticed he had gained a companion. The little crab shaped watcher and viewer were not randomly wandering. They were following him. Tomm stopped at the side of the freeway and sat for a moment allowing the little machines to get closer. The viewer was slow to respond, but came to him.

Tomm had heard tale of the things. They looked hideous, and he was not about to touch it, but it turned around and let him see the picture on it's back.

"John!" He gasped seeing his long lost lover.

John was bound and gagged and was being roughly escorted off of a jet. Tomm watched helplessly as John was kicked and shoved mercilessly toward a car. Then the screen went black as a can was dropped over the top of whatever watcher was seeing it happen.

"But where is he?" Tomm asked the viewer, crying now. Where is my husband?"

The little screen flickered and the viewer changed frequency and found a new watcher.

A sign appeared, Mexico City, 3 miles. Then the little machine scurried off. Tomm was on his feet in an instant. He would need a car.

Finding a car was easy. With so many people in camps there were houses left empty and it took no time for Tomm to break into one, find the car keys, and be off. He was lucky enough to find a little cash in his plundering. He felt bad, but he felt even worse that the

previous owner had been ushered away to
a camp where they wouldn't even be able
to enjoy the fruits of their life
labors.

The freeways were also fairly
uncontested, and the beginnings of the
trip started so sweetly. Tomm was
drowning with concern for John, but
driving relaxed him and he was just
watching the scenery go by. It was nice
since he had spent so much time with no
scenery. He was so lost in his quiet
thoughts that the lights didn't
immediately register. The siren snapped
him out of it though.

"Fuck!" He spat out as he realized
he was being pulled over.

Tomm pulled over to the side as he
didn't want to start too much of a
stir. He wasn't sure what to do. The
highway patrol car pulled up behind and
braked to a stop. Tomm rolled down his
window.

The officer waited a rather long
time before getting out of his vehicle
and approaching Tomm's.

"Can I see your license please?" The
officer asked as he came to the window.

"I must have left it home." Tomm
quickly lied.

"Are there any weapons in the car?"

"No sir."

"Step out of the car please."

"Do you want to tell me why I'm being pulled over officer?"

"Standard with anyone on the road anymore. New procedure sent directly from the government. Step out of the car please."

"Apparently there isn't a need for a reason anymore." Tomm thought to himself.

As Tomm stepped out of the car he became suddenly aware of his slovenly state. Living in the streets had left him a bit on the unshaven and dirty side.

"Put your hands on the hood of the car and place your legs shoulder length apart."

Tomm did as he was told.

"I'm going to search you. Are you carrying any weapons?"

"No sir."

The officer's hands began to brush over Tomm. They were strong, but surprisingly gentle. They moved with purpose. Tomm was reminded of his past fantasies about cops. His erection couldn't be controlled. The officer stopped for a second noticing, but moved along with the search.

"Looks like you're clean but I need you to come with me to my car please."

"Do you mind telling me why?"

"Just come without a struggle." The officer said. "Please." He sounded strange. Something was up, but without any aggression on his part the glow bug remained unresponsive. The man clearly meant Tomm no ill.

"After you." The officer said, motioning Tomm toward the police car.

"No cuffs?" Tomm mumbled.

"Do we need any?" The officer replied.

When they reached the patrol car the officer opened the back door and motioned Tomm inside. Tomm was hesitant but got in. The door clicked to a close as the officer pressed on it.

"Great going dork." Tomm thought to himself. *"Lot of good you're going to do in jail."*

The officer climbed into the driver's seat and closed the door.

"You want to tell me what you're doing?" The officer asked.

"What do you mean?" Tomm responded hoping that playing dumb would get him out of this mess.

"Cut the crap. I know that isn't your car. So where you going in a stolen car?"

"It's not…"

"It's stolen! It belongs to a very close friend of mine. That's why I pulled you over. I was hoping it was he inside but look what I found instead. He couldn't have given you permission to use it. They got him."

"They?" Tomm asked. He was feeling a little confused now. What was the officer reaching for? If he had known the car was stolen why didn't he just make the arrest? It would have made things so easy. The aggressive force of it would have put him in the gutter, and Tomm would have been on his way.

"God Damn it! Stop playing dumb! The street patrol took him to a camp for queers!"

Things were moving around in Tomm's head now. He was beginning to understand.

"Now you gonna tell me what's up or you gonna sit back there and think it over while I haul your ass in. How did you end up in my man's car? What are you running from?"

"I'm not…"

"Like hell you're not running away. It's obvious."

The car was silent for a while. Tomm was thinking.

"I guess I need to take you in then." The officer said starting the car.

"Okay, okay, I'll tell you." Tomm said trying to delay the trip to jail. "I stole it."

"I already know that, but why? You trying to get away from that bitch and her army? I wish we had run. I would have had him for a while longer."

Tomm heard the pain in the man's voice and sat a moment stunned in disbelief. His luck was amazing. He decided to tell the man the truth, part of it at least.

"I'm going to Mexico, but I'm really not running. I'm going to break my man out of a camp."

The Officer turned around to look through the screen between them abruptly.

"Are you crazy! There are loads of roadblocks on the way, and what makes you think you'll get to him when you make it there. They have hundreds of men on lookout. I know. I checked into it."

"I have a secret weapon." Tomm said vaguely.

"You said you had no weapons." The officer said sounding startled. His dark eyes looked Tomm up and down suspiciously and not entirely without fear.

"It's not what you would expect." Tomm said honestly.

"Will it work?"

"Without a doubt."

"Show me?" The officer said questioningly, the tenor coming back into his voice.

"Why should I show you? So you can take me in? So you can stop me?"

"If it is good enough to convince me that you can do what you say you can then I will go with you. I'll help."

Tomm sat in stunned silence again for a moment. How could he show the man? The bug was totally visible to the naked eye, but it required aggression to activate. This man meant him no ill.

"I'll show you. Let me out of the car."

The officer got out and opened the back door. Tomm got out and stood up.

"See the little fire fly on me? That's the weapon."

"You're joking."

"Nope."

"What does it do?"

"It protects me."

"That is the stupidest thing I have ever heard. Do you think I'm an idiot?"

Tomm rolled his eyes and shook his head. "Hit me."

"What the hell are you talking about?"

"You have to hit me to make it work."

The officer reached out and lightly punched Tomm on the arm. Nothing happened.

"So what now?" The officer asked sarcastically.

"You have to intend it to hurt, but don't get too into it for your own safety."

"Okay." The officer said. He closed his eyes as if to brace himself then pulled his arm back took aim and started to take a swing. His arm stopped in mid swing. His eyes rolled back and he fell to his knees clutching his head.

"God Damn!" The officer looked up at Tomm. His eyes were bloodshot. "What the hell just happened?"

"The more violence you intend the worse the pain. It even works against guns, and as far as I can tell it doesn't matter how far away the other person is." Tomm explained.

"How did you get this thing?"

"I'm not sure, but I have my ideas, I think it was made by my husband. He's an inventor. He's the one who invented the armor no one can break. The government stole it from him. I think he invented the watchers and their all-telling counterparts. He's the man I'm going to break out of the camps."

"I'm in, but we need a less suspicious mode of travel. The car you stole is also listed as owned by the government as well as any property formerly owned by prisoners. We take mine."

Tomm smiled at his good fortune. He wasn't used to things going his way.

"Climb in, but get in the front seat this time. My name's Jim Beau."

"My name's Tomm."

Tomm climbed in and Jim Beau started the car. In a moment they were turned around and headed back into the city.

Jim Beau's house was set in the back of a very quiet dead end street. For that Tomm was thankful.

"Come inside." Jim Beau said after they had climbed out of his patrol car, so inside they went.

"We need to leave as little to question as possible when we leave. I'm going back to work. I'm gonna take a sick leave and drop off the car and I'll be back. Take a shower and clean up. I'll be back soon."

Jim Beau turned around and left. He looked exited to be about this rebellion. He didn't look too sick, but Tomm hoped he was a good actor. The door clicked shut and Tomm started his search for the bathroom. It didn't take long. He found a clean towel in the closet, and there was a new razor in a drawer. He hoped Jim-Beau wouldn't mind.

Tomm stripped off his clothes and started the warm water in the shower. He looked himself over in the mirror. The Suzy Q Sue had branded into his cheek didn't show too clearly with his beard as long as it was. Tomm was surprised at how muscular he had become. He was quite the specimen. He

had always admired his own dick. It was
incredibly thick. Good big round balls
too. It mad most men jealous. He wasn't
as long as his husband though. He
missed John. He longed to be held by
him.

Tomm stepped into the shower and let
the refreshing warmth of water run over
him. He reached for the soap and began
a much needed clean up. The suds felt
incredibly good. He turned the
showerhead away so he could soap up
everywhere. The slick soap did its job,
and his big hands rubbed it in. He
spent a little extra time rubbing it
into the hair under his arms and inside
his butt crack then lathering it around
on his belly and around his balls. His
hands sliding over his dick made it
instantly erect but he didn't linger.
He pulled the showerhead back toward
him and rinsed off all the soap and
grime of weeks passed and let it wash
away and down the drain. Then he turned
off the water.

The towel was soft and smelled of
fabric softener. The terry cloth soaked
up the water quickly. Tomm hung the
towel up and then went to work on his
beard. He used the razor to trim under
his neck and on his cheeks. It
immediately made the Suzy Q halfway
visible. He would have to trim the rest
so the Suzy Q wouldn't look too

strange, although it would be impossible to explain anyway.

There was a pair of trimmers in the top drawer. He plugged them in and found the right attachment and trimmed away. They made his beard look very distinguished. The Suzy Q showed damn clearly, angry and red, which was how he felt when he looked at it. He would take his life back from that bitch. She couldn't hurt him anymore. He felt invincible.

"Uhh humm…" Tomm heard. He hadn't thought to close the bathroom door. He turned to see Jim Beau staring at him and his still half erect dick dangling largely between his legs.

"You're a incredible looking man." Jim Beau said quietly.

Tomm smiled looking Jim Beau up and down. There was an obvious tent in the man's pants.

"Thank you." Tomm said getting another hard on. He reached down and tugged once.

Jim Beau stepped a little closer but was hesitant to touch.

Tomm closed the gap, taking Jim Beau's hand and placing it on his chest.

Jim Beau's fingers ran shaking through the thick dark hair there down toward Tomm's dick.

Tomm's fingers made busy unbuttoning Jim Beaus shirt and pants then unzipping them.

Jim Beau pulled his shirt off the rest of the way, shrugging it to the floor then wasted no time dropping his drawers.

Tomm dropped to his knees and quickly had his mouth on Jim Beau's dick. He sucked it all in right to the thick hair around it. Jim Beau's dick was not incredibly long but was thick and covered in pulsing veins. His balls, which were pressed tightly into Tomm's chin, were big and round and covered with thick dark hair. It didn't look much different from Tomm's.

Tomm was lost in the moment. His tongue gliding over the soft bumpy surface skin of Jim Beau's dick, saliva dripping off of his chin.

Jim Beau was thrusting hard, his hands behind Tomm's head pulling it into his him.

Tomm's hands were clutching Jim Beau's buttocks forcing the motion and Tomm's dick was slapping against the floor with their rhythm. Tomm wanted to be fucked. He had rarely wanted it this badly. It must have been his reminiscence of John. He turned around on his hands and knees turning his ass into the air with his desire for a dick to fill it up.

Jim Beau didn't hesitate and dropped
to his knees. His dick was wet with
saliva from Tomm mouth, and he pressed
it against the sweet spot softly.

Tomm was ready and it slid inside
him wonderfully, warmly. He could feel
Jim Beau's huge balls pressed against
him and knew the man was all the way
in.

Jim Beau mounted strongly, and
fucked with the fury of months of fear
and loneliness behind him. It stretched
and filled Tomm and massaged and
tickled him where he needed it. The
passion of it drove him to his stomach.
Jim Beau didn't miss a beat. He rolled
forward and pressed his hands heavily
onto Tomm's shoulder blades keeping him
from moving. Keeping him self in
complete control, and he let loose.

"Aahhhh! Yeah." Jim Beau groaned
watching his own quick thrusts plunge
in and out of Tomm's very hairy ass.
The rings of Tomm's anus pulling ever
so slightly out with each withdrawal as
it hugged tightly around Jim Beau's
dick.

He knew he was going to cum soon and
was surprised to feel the twitching of
Tomm's ass around his dick which meant
that the man had came from getting
fucked. It threw him over the top and
he drove his dick home hard and fast
shooting months of saved up semen deep

into Tomm's ass. He fell on top of the
man savoring the reminiscent throbbing
of a spent erection and held Tomm close
not moving and not pulling free for a
long time, just enjoying the feeling of
a man wrapped around his dick, and the
connection of the warm body underneath
him.

After a long time just lying there
Jim Beau started again, his erection
renewed. This time slowly and softly,
the whole time kissing the back of
Tomm's neck.

"I miss you so much John." Tomm
thought between groans. *"This will be
you and me soon."*

Unseen his glow bug split and grew
into two complete glow bugs. One
attached to Tomm and a new one attached
to Jim Beau.

It took a few minutes to clean up
after they recovered from the pleasant
exhaustion of a good time. The rest of
the after noon was spent loading the
automobile with sleeping bags, clean
clothes, and food.

There wouldn't be time to stop, and
the world was a little different since
Sue's militant takeover. They would
stop for gas, but they would make their
stops as short as possible, and try to
stay as unnoticed as possible.

They took to the road in the early
evening, and Tomm took the first
driving shift. The miles flew by, and
they were somewhat hypnotic. There were
others on the road, but there were
mostly only transport and delivery
vehicles. Sue didn't want to shut the
world down, but wanted unnecessary
travel squelched. It was easier to stop
a rebellion if you knew where people
were. Besides she didn't want her
populace to starve, and she needed a
stable economy. Still she had begun to
put a permit for long distance travel
policy into play. Tomm and Jim Beau
would have to deal with that
eventually.

It wasn't until a few days later
that the secret of the glow bugs became
totally revealed.

Tomm and Jim Beau pulled into a
small gas station to fuel up. Jim Beau
stepped out of the 2003 Churvy
Sunburnban and there was a note posted.

"Please pre pay for all gas
purchases." It read.

Jim Beau stepped inside to pay the
clerk. The clerk eyed him up and down.

"You from around here?" The clerk
queried.

"No I'm headed south."

"You have a permit for travel?"

"What do you mean?" Jim Beau was a
bit set back.

"I can't sell gas to non locals unless they have a permit to travel long distances. It's the law."

"I'll go elsewhere then." Jim Beau responded.

"You see that's where the trouble lies. I can't let you leave here without the local authorities checking you out either. It's the law." The clerk leaned forward threateningly.

"You think you can stop me?"

"Maybe not me, but Betsy can." The clerk said as he pulled a rifle from behind the counter.

Jim Beau immediately leapt for the door. He had been through enough training as an officer of the law to know better than to give the man time to aim. He almost made it out of the door before he heard the man screaming.

The rifle fell to the floor. "Thunk."

"Ahhh! Fuck! My back!" The clerk was screaming as he began falling to the floor. "What the fuck did you do to my back?" Then the clerk passed out.

Jim Beau's little glow bug danced into then back out of his vision. It was the first time he had seen it.

Jim Beau smiled. He knew what had happened. "You tried to shoot me in the back you stupid son of a bitch! Like a fucking coward."

The little bell attached to the door jingled as Tomm came into the little store to see what was taking so long. His eyes landed on the little glow bug dancing around Jim Beau's head. He looked around thinking it had been his and saw that there were in fact two.

"I have one now too." Jim Beau smiled at Tomm. "I don't know how but I have one."

It was slowly clicking into place in Tomm's head now. He was remembering the alley where he had fucked a stranger with another man. He remembered seeing a little glow bug leave with one of them, but he had convinced himself that it had been his own.

"I think its because we had sex." Tomm said still trying to remember.

"You think?" Jim Beau asked.

"There's one way to find out for sure." Tomm said.

"What are you saying?"

"We find a man, fuck him, and see if he ends up with one."

"You're kidding right?"

"No, but before you get weird just hear me out." Tomm paused. "Before I met you there was one other sexual experience I had. It was in an alley with two other men. I had all out sex with one of them, and I think that I saw a glow bug following him out of the alley when he left."

"You sure?" Jim Beau asked. "We risk exposing ourselves."

"What's wrong? You not up for a little fun?" Tomm challenged. "Besides, what they gonna do about it? No one can touch us."

"You suggesting rape?"

"Hell no!" Tomm flushed. "We just find men who are alone and hit on them until one consents. The ones who are offended won't be able to touch us. They'll just end up with head shattering pain. Also just think about what this means. When we get to the camp not only can we set John free but we can set all of the men free and no one will be able to lock them up again."

"Not to mention being able to be absolutely 100% gay with no fear of punishment." Jim Beau said smiling now, a big ear to ear grin. "I can hit on any man I think is attractive and no one can do a fucking thing about it."

Tomm smiled as the idea took hold. "This is gonna be one hell of a road trip."

"You bet your sweet ass it is." Jim Beau's eyes gleamed.

"First we fill up with gas though. I'll go set the pump."

After filling up the Sunburnban the two pulled away from the station and headed for town. The first three men

were a total bust. It was a small town
and the men had probably never been
directly hit on before. All three of
them reacted violently which downed
them with whatever special pain the
glow bug created. Tomm felt a little
badly for them but he reminded himself
that all it was doing was
incapacitating them and making them
feel exactly what they intended to do
to him.

The fourth man, however, smiled
instead. He was a young man, probably
around twenty four. He had a very nice
tan and the build of a hard worker.

Jim Beau pointed him out. He was out
mowing the lawn with his shirt off.
Tomm pulled the Sunburnban to the curb
and the two men stepped out of the car
and onto the sidewalk next to his house
ogling the man up and down.

"Can I help you gentlemen?" The man
asked after he stopped the mower and
stepped over to where they were. "You
need directions?"

"No need for directions." Jim Beau
said. "That's not what we stopped for."

"We were just admiring you." Tomm
said. "You are stunningly handsome."

The man looked around nervously and
blushed a deep red.

"Well, thank you…" He said.

"It's damn hot out today. You got a
drink for a few wayward men?" Jim Beau

asked. Tomm smiled. Jim Beau had a way
with words.

"Sure, I have a few beers inside if
you're interested." The man said. He
was noticeably shaking with excitement.
Tomm had a feeling this sort of thing
didn't happen to him very often.

"Is the misses home?" Tomm asked.

"I don't have a misses. Not for lack
of her tryin though. I got a girl,
sorta." The man shrugged. It made his
muscles bunch nicely around his
shoulders on his back. "She's working
today."

The inside of the house was clean
and smelled like home cooking. The man
left Tomm and Jim Beau in the front
room and stepped toward where they
assumed the kitchen was. Tomm heard the
fridge door open and close. The man
came back with three cold beers. He
passed them out and opened his own
taking a big gulp.

"You're right. It was hot out. I
needed a break." The man said now
taking the time to look Tomm and Jim
Beau over.

Tomm stepped to the man and leaned
in giving the man a firm kiss. Jim Beau
acted on the signal stepping in from
behind the man kissing his neck while
his hands reached around front and
unbuttoned and unzipped the man's jeans
pulling them down a little so he could

get hold of some dick. Jim Beau loved the feel of a young man's skin.

This man had been outside in the heat and his nuts were hanging incredibly low, the weight of them rolling in his hands felt nice. His dick was a good man's size, and it was hard as hell sticking straight out toward Tomm who was going to his knees.

Tomm slipped his mouth around that dick smoothly.

Jim Beau dropped behind the man and started tounging his other side.

"Ahhh… Yeah…" The man groaned as he relaxed and started to enjoy what was happening. Both Tomm and Jim Beau wasted no time stripping off their shirts and undoing their pants so they could get at their own hard dicks. The pittery pattery sounds of the two men jacking off filled the air next to the groans of the man in the middle.

Tomm decided it was time and stood up and bent over giving the man access to his wet, ready ass. The man smiled and stepped into it, slipping solidly and a little too quickly inside. Tomm flinched but forced himself to relax. It worked and in seconds he was groaning as the man started thrusting.

Jim Beau had a similar idea and since he had tongued the man's ass and wetted it he stood behind the man. He spit into his hand and used it to

lubricate his own dick and then pressed
himself against the man.

"Go slow." The man said. "It's been
a long time."

Jim Beau understood and massaged the
man's hole with the wet head of his
dick gently, pressing it in a little
then letting it slip back until he
could tell the man was ready then he
slid it slowly and steadily into the
man's ass.

"Mmmm. Fuckin A." The man said as he
set the rhythm making sure his dick
stayed inside Tomm and Jim Beau's dick
stayed inside of him as he rocked back
and forward. "Ahhh… I'm gonna shoot."
He groaned.

"Shoot it baby." Tomm said pressing
his ass back into the man. "Fill my
hungry hole up with your cum boy."

The man did. Jim Beau could feel his
anus tightening and relaxing around his
stiff meat. It was all it took. He was
so exited he blew his load without
warning, thrusting hard and out of
control, unable to hold back.

"Yeah!" Jim Beau grunted as his wad
shot up and out of his dick and into
the man's ass.

"You cumin too?" The man asked back
at him.

"Oh yeah! I'm cumin hard." Jim Beau
said.

The weight of the two men pressed
against Tomm forcing the Man's dick
deep and caused the man's low hanging
balls to swing up slapping Tomm's own
swinging nuts. He was jerking it hard
and fast and the feel of that soft skin
slapping his balls sent him over the
top. He came and watched his own ropey
jets of cum shoot out of his big dick
across the floor in front of him.

"Oh yeah." He said as his legs
shivered under him with the pleasure of
releasing that load.

The man slowly pulled out behind him
and Tomm tried to hold the cum in, but
it ejected from his ass and it dripped
down the inside of his leg. He liked
cum and pulled his pants up relishing
the feel of it soaking into the fabric
of his jeans.

Tomm turned around to see Jim Beau
stuffing his thick half hard dick back
into his pants and zipping them up. He
stepped back for a more complete
picture watching Jim Beau's glow bug as
it lighted gently on top of the man's
head and then split in two. The two
halves quickly grew into two complete
glow bugs.

"So it's true then." He said to Jim
Beau not thinking to explain to the
man.

Jim Beau nodded.

"What's true?" The man asked.

"I'd say we owe an explanation." Jim Beau said to Tomm. "Don't want to leave the man in the dark."

"I'm Tomm." Tomm introduced himself. "And this is Jim Beau." He added introducing them both.

"I'm Chris." The man introduced himself. "What explanation?" He asked pulling up his pants, zipping them and buttoning them. He recovered his beer, and sat down on the sofa. Tomm and Jim Beau joined him.

As if knowing they would be the topic of conversation the glow bugs began circling the air above them drawing Chris's attention.

"Hang on I'll get a fly swatter. How'd those buggers get in here anyway?"

"Wait." Tomm said. "They aren't normal bugs. Try to catch one."

Chris tried to catch one but found himself feeling queasy and light headed, and had to sit down.

"What's going on here?" He asked.

"Tell him the whole story." Jim Beau said to Tomm. "All of it."

So Tomm told him about the glow bugs, about his John, and about how he came to meet Jim Beau. He left out his affiliation with Sue. He didn't want to scare either of them off with his outlaw status. He figured it luck that

he hadn't been found out yet. He hoped
his luck would hold.

"So you're going to save as many
gays as possible?" Chris asked.

"As many as I can."

"And to save them you must fuck
them?"

"It appears that it is my calling, a
spiritual and moral obligation really."
Tomm chuckled at the irony.

"So you're telling me that it is, in
our case, immoral not to fuck as many
willing men as we possibly can, and
that by doing so we will save the world
from that bitch who has declared
herself our world president?"

"You got it." Jim Beau affirmed."

"I have one question. Where do I
sign up?" Chris laughed. "You got room
for one more?"

They helped Chris pack up a sleeping
bag pillow and a few clothes, restocked
the cooler in the sunburnban, then sat
and waited for Chris's girl to get
home.

"You sure she won't freak?" Tomm
asked again for the fifth time.

"She isn't gonna freak. I told you
she moved in with me to throw off the
damn morality police. I have a man of
my own, I hope. His name is Larry. She
knew him too and after he was arrested
she moved in here to keep em from
getting me. She's a good strong woman,

and she'll understand. Although I have
to admit she is a bit taken with me."
Chris explained. "So stop worrying."

Chris got up and went into the
kitchen to get another beer.

"He's a fine looking man to take on
this trip." Jim Beau said.

"Try and save some for your new
found purpose in life." Tomm said.

"Hmmm. It's gonna be hard."

"I certainly hope it will be. I hope
it'll stay good and hard. We're gonna
need it." Tomm laughed.

The front door opened just as Chris
was returning with three beers in hand.
A rather attractive woman stared in.
She had long dark hair and green eyes,
and she was definitely startled to see
men in the house.

"Chris? What the hell you up to the
house smells like sex! You told me you
were gonna be careful. What the hell
are we gonna do if the guard show up
diggin up your past? Why you have to
get all horny now? You think we don't
have enough problems with all our
snooping neighbors?"

"Carrie, These two gents are Tomm,"
Chris said gesturing to him, "and Jim
Beau." Chris gestured to the other.
"We're gonna go break out Larry."

"What the hell! You are even crazier
than I thought and as for you two why
the hell you goading this ox brained

idiot on like that? There have got to
be thousands of guards watching each
one of those camps. Who the hell are
you to be leading him on this wild
goose chase?" Her face had gotten
terribly red.

"Baby watch that temper, we have
guests." Chris said.

Carrie drew back her hand to slap
him.

"Ahhh!!!" She screamed as his glow
bug reacted.

She looked around stunned.

"How did you do that Chris? I swear
to God you just slapped me good and
hard, but you didn't move an inch."

"Carrie, sit down and breathe for a
moment and for God's sake be quiet for
long enough to hear an explanation."
Chris said calmly. "I'm gonna need your
help."

Carrie grabbed Chris's beer from him
and sat down on the end of the sofa.
She took a big drink and touched her
cheek as if it had been struck.

"Well? I'm listening."

The explanation was brief and by the
end of it Carrie was convinced of its
eminent success.

"You make sure he eats good food."
She said as the three men left. "Or
there'll be hell to pay."

The road trip went faster now that
there were three of them. They talked
it over and all agreed that they didn't
want the camp guards to know they were
coming. Surprise was in their favor. So
they kept a low profile and avoided
people and places that would get them
caught. They were wanted men now, and
if the prison camp knew what they were
up to there was no doubt in any of
their minds that they would arrive to
find the place vacant of life but full
of death.

There were a few times when they
were pulled over, and they did their
best to get out of the situation
without hurting anyone.

The aggressive police officers
downed themselves. The few non-
aggressive ones simply let it go as a
warning. One or two were even the proud
owners of glow bugs themselves after
the encounters.

There was a big stretch of highway
between the northeastern United States
and Mexico City. Most of it was desert
and the three stopped frequently to get
food and buy gas. They had worked out a
system now.

Chris it turned out was a very nice
asset to have along. Not only was
having a third man along the thing that
deterred most of the officers out
looking for the two wanted men, but it

was his idea that kept them with a full
tank. They were just around the
California border on highway 10 when
the tank got low enough that a refill
was needed.

"How are we going to get fuel
without the entire countries police
force coming for us. We were lucky back
there when we picked up Chris and with
all of the men we hit on there I'm sure
that they have a pretty good
description of us." Tomm said as they
pulled off the freeway and over to the
side of the road to discuss their
circumstances.

"It's not a big deal. We are already
spreading the bug. We just get them to
fuel us up too. We just rely on the
local gay boys to take care of it.
Might not be a bad idea to switch cars
as well." Chris said. "Just leave it up
to me."

Chapter Nineteen

In the Future

Trapped "Meow… Meow, Meow, Meow."

"Make no mistake. It's about power. It has always been about power. The battle between good and evil, all that transpires, all that exists is about power. What you should be concerned with is who has that power and weather or not you want them to have it. Ultimately if they have the power you don't."

"Where are you going with this?" Harvey asked.

"You don't believe completely yet, but you are a fledgling God. Not only that but you are a new kind of God. Currently you are full of potential but not full of power. The power that lies waiting for you is your birthright but you must claim it. Others have already begun to snatch it away. You will have to find ways to get it under your control and out of theirs." Mars said.

"Will you go with me?"

"No my boy. This quest is yours and I am old and weary. I sense a rebirth

for myself but until it comes I will
sleep."

The fire crackled and the crickets
chirped in the night. Harvey sat
thinking.

"Who will guide me?"

"You must guide yourself. It is your
quest. I will tell you where to start
though. My old lab is close now and
that is where I will find rest. Under
my lab, through the cellar you will
find a network of caves. That is where
you must go. Somewhere in that network
of caves deep under ground there is an
opening that only you will recognize.
It is the entrance to the labyrinth."

"Labyrinth?"

"All planets have one. Just as all
planets have a God entity. Gia is the
manifestation of this planets mind,
heart and soul, just as I am the
manifestation of Mars. You must find
where your God link comes from."

Harvey nodded starting to
understand.

"Understand me when I tell you,
Harvey, that this has never happened
before, you going from man to God. When
a planet is born, a God is born within
it. There is no new planet. You are
something new and unique. It is
troubling. We must learn what happened
and do it quickly. You are in a great
deal of danger. There are other Gods to

deal with and they are jealous of
power. They will come looking for this
new power they feel."

"Why do we wait then?"

"You have cast your first God Spell.
I felt it and know it was real. You
have summoned something to us and we
must wait for it to get here."

The jungle was damp and they waited
there in the dark, God and God-ling
together. Harvey was tired and as the
night progressed his mind wandered
until it found sleep. All the time
wondering, *Why Me? Nothing special
here."*

"Cats? Hsst...phtt...meow...squeak..." Gia
managed as she found herself wound
tightly into the God-ling's new and
first God Spell. "He made me a cat!"
She hissed and growled. "Not only a cat
but a male cat!" Gia was pissed.

Trista purred contented. "He chose
kittens." She purred.

Soft white fur covered her and a
downy silver mane of kitten hair ringed
her neck. Gia was her twin brother. The
only noticeable difference was the
color of their eyes. Trista's eyes were
gold while Gia's eyes were a brilliant
emerald green.

Trista loved cats, and from a
witches perspective being reborn a cat
was not a bad thing but a good thing,

not only that but she had always
wondered what it felt like being male.
She squinted through her yellow eyes at
the night. She was starving and
couldn't smell her mother near by. She
knew also both instinctively and from
her memory as a witch that she must
find Harvey or die from hunger or from
the attack of predators.

"Come brother we must find him or
perish." Trista meowed.

"I'll stay here!" Gia growled
defiantly.

Trista almost casually reached out
and scratched Gia across the nose.

"Ouch! You know what I'll do to
you?" The once Goddess yelped.

"Do try." Trista purred. "Being a
Goddess made things easy for you, but
me having been a witch, I know more
about the rules."

"My power!" Gia screeched as the
tried to cast a God Spell. "What have
you done to my power witch?"

Gia had reached for her power and
found it, yet it sat un-responsive,
gleaming but out of reach.

"Not I." Trista purred triumphantly.
"Harvey..."

"I can't live without my power." Gia
mewed unhappily.

"My magic won't work either." Trista
meowed. "It is part of familiar law."

"Explain!" Gia demanded with a hiss.

"Cat's are familiars. It is in their nature."

"What, pray tell, is a familiar?" Gia asked in a series of low garbled meows.

"When a witch encounters a particularly troublesome demon, or summons one to powerful to control, or maybe even one too young to have learned to control their own rage, she can place it inside the body of a familiar. There it will remain trapped and enslaved indefinitely, it's power locked unless it's witch says it can use it and then only very specifically for what it's witch says the power can be used for."

"I am his slave?" Gia whimpered miserably.

"I find it ironic since until very recently I was your slave my brother. Now we are equals."

"Why must we go to him then? Just to do what he says?" Gia meowed.

"If we don't go to him we will die from exposure not to mention the magical repercussions."

"Please explain." Gia meowed, starting to settle down now.

"We must taste the blood of the witch who entrapped us by sunrise before the first rays of morning touch us for no other thing can nourish us from this moment on. No food but his blood will work. Only a drop is needed. After we feed on it we will be sustained and fed by his life force until the spell is broke, or we are dead, whichever one comes first. So you see there are perks." Meow… meuw… mrr… mrr… Trista warbled her explanation.

"So when he dies we are free?"

"Oh no. You don't want that. Break the spell sure if you have a body to go to, but in the event of his death our spirits are permanently linked to those of the cats we are inside of and we will be forced to follow them into the next life. I'm sorry Gia, but you will never be entirely free of this should he die. You must protect him until he chooses to free you or you will forfeit you place of power. This is why demons fear the power of human witches so much. Witches have the power to make them mortal. It's never been done to a God before though."

"Sounds foolish to me." Gia grumbled.

"I didn't make the rules." Trista purred.

"I would like to scratch whoever did." Gia meowed.

"Let's go then." Trista purred, and the two twin kittens slipped into the jungle night, making very little noise.

"Where is he then?" Gia asked.

"You can't feel him?" Trista was surprised.

"I can't." Gia growled.

"Hmmm. It must work differently for all, the perks of familiarity." Trista meowed. "I can feel him close by. We will be there soon. Just stay on my tail."

"I'm following aren't I?" Gia grumbled.

"One more thing." Trista meowed.

"What's that?" Gia meowed back.

"He won't know we need to take a bite so we'll have to sneak up on him and take a good hard bite to get the blood we need. I never taught him the ways of witches. The power almost always skips boys."

"Biting him will make me very happy." Gia purred, imagining the hunt and attack on her imposed master.

Mars watched with curiosity as the two little lion cubs crouched and snuck up on the sleeping Harvey, creeping on their bellies. The God Spell had altered their color. He had never seen such strange looking lion cubs. White with silver manes was not exactly the safest color for jungle animals. They were cute little things though. He watched, wondering what would happen.

The two little cubs crawled up to Harvey's exposed hand then, in unison, they both bit his hand hard enough to draw blood.

"Yeow!" Harvey yelled. "What the hell?"

The jungle fell silent.

"A cat?" Mars laughed as his God sight showed him what had transpired. "You have made a Goddess into a cat?"

Gia hissed at Mars, her green eyes gleaming.

"This is a most fitting solution for a very dangerous problem."

"What do you know Mars?" Gia growled.

"*I am your older brother Gia and have taken my time learning about some of these things.*" Mars let his God power speak to Gia. "*We must talk later. There is much you need to know about your new form. I will be happy to teach you all that I know of this.*"

"*Trista has enlightened me some.*" Gia meowed. "*But I would like any help you could lend.*"

"What is going on?" Harvey asked.

"This one is Gia. Mars said intoning toward the green eyes cub. "But who is the other?"

Mars reached over and took the little yellow-eyed cub into his arms to look into its eyes while Harvey rubbed at his recently bitten hand. The cub immediately began to purr.

"Trista?" Mars asked.

"Meow?" Trista responded.

"My mother?" Harvey asked beginning now to understand his fever dreams and what had nearly killed him.

"My boy, I knew you had summoned something to us in order to save yourself. I had no idea you had summoned your enemies, the same ones from whom we were running, and not only that but you have made them your allies. A very clever solution." Mars's voice was filled with pride.

"You mean those vicious little fur balls are Gia and my mother?"

"Yes Harvey, they are."

"Why aren't we running then?"

"Because when you stuck then into the bodies of kitten's you rendered them harmless to us."

"How?" Harvey asked still rubbing his hand. Mars took Harvey's hand to heal the bleeding bite marks.

"I will tell you a story." Mars said. "Gia needs to hear it too. It is a bit of history really. It's the reason cat's were worshiped and also the reason Gods refuse, under any circumstances to use cats for host bodies. We call them the guardians to the gates of the dead. They hold the keys to the doors between this life and the next.

"Meow." Trista said.

"Trista knows this, a little of it,
at least it seems." Mars continued...

Chapter Twenty

Past and Present

Prison Break

By the time Tomm reached the prison encampment he had recruited only around thirty men to his cause but they had left behind them hundreds of men who now possessed glow bugs and were happily going about the business of spreading them around.

Tomm was on a mission though. He needed to find John, his husband who was in a great deal of danger, waiting for his lover to rescue him from somewhere inside a prison for who the, she bitch, world president considered deviants in her slanted opinion.

"You know what to do men." Tomm said to his newfound friends.

"Fuck em all... Fuck em all..." They whispered in unison.

"Tell every one you give a glow bug to what you know and encourage them to do the same. By morning there needs to be a glow bug attached to every willing man inside those walls."

"Fuck em all..." The men whispered
again. It had, over the last few weeks
become a battle cry. They all had their
big guns. They just weren't the type
for killing.

The siege on the prison compound was
quiet and incredibly easy. The glow
bugs rendered the guards unconscious
the moment they lifted their weapons.

Tomm started by finding keys to the
men's cells on one of the downed
guards. Then with his band of horny men
they made their way toward the
prisoners.

Tomm found himself quickly
rethinking strategy though when they
encountered the first of them. He
hadn't entirely been prepared for the
grizzly condition the prisoners were
in. The prisoners were dirty, beaten,
and starving. These men were in no
condition for sex.

"Change of plans men."

"What?" the men responded.

"These men are in no state for love
making. Let's just get them cleaned and
fed and then worry about getting them
out of here. The fucking can come later
for those who are interested."

"What should we do then?" Jim Beau
piped in.

"Let's find the prison showers to
start. I think a warm shower and some

clean cloths is the right place to
start if it can be arranged."

"Where do you suppose the showers
are?" Jim Beau asked.

"Your guess is as good as mine.
Maybe if we ask one of the prisoners
they will know."

"We should gag and tie the downed
guards you know. They could start some
trouble if they come to and call for
reinforcements." Jim Beau suggested.

"I agree. Lets go to it men." Tomm
said. He went to open the first cell.
The man had seen them and was sitting
against the wall staring.

"You aint guards." He said beginning
to pick up on what was happening. Tomm
unlocked the cell.

"Nope, we're your ticket out of
here."

The man walked weakly to the door.
Tomm wasted no time lending his arm to
help support the man.

"Didn't think I'd ever taste freedom
again. Figured I'd die here in this
place from starvation, or worse."

Tomm could tell the man had been
rugged and handsome once, probably a
farm hand or something like it. Now the
man was gangly and beaten.

"Do you know your way to the
showers?" Tomm asked.

"Yeah, but the guards will see us
coming."

"Let us worry about the guards. Trust me your safe."

"I'll show you. It's down by the mess hall."

"Good, maybe we can get some food cooked too then." Tomm said as they started for the next cell.

"Amazing." The man said as they encountered another guard who attempted to pull up his firearm and then fell limp to the floor, unconscious. "What countries military are you? Who decided to help us?"

"We aren't the military." Tomm said. "We are just men like yourself. We have all lost lovers who were sent here and we came to get them back."

"How did you defeat the guard?"

"I will explain after the work is done and everyone is safe." Tomm promised.

The cells were emptied and the men were freed down to the last man. There were men who didn't make it. The camp conditions were just too terrible and many were sick and might still not make it, but even with the sadness of such loss everyone's spirits were up with hope of freedom and an end to the atrocities they had suffered.

The guards could be found in the mess hall as well. They were bound and gagged. Some of them were regaining consciousness, but most were still out cold.

The newly free men were happy to go to the showers to clean up and get some fresh clothing although all that could be found were the plain prisoner jumpsuits which were standard clothing here.

They couldn't find a lot of variety in the kitchen for meals, but there were potatoes and hams. They went to work making hash and hoped that it would help the men a little more. They had still to get away from here.

Tomm was still searching for his lost husband but he felt that it was more important to feed the hungry first. The men shoveled it down and in no time there was a quiet chattering between the men. Tomm knew that the time had come for explanations.

Tomm stood on a table so that everyone would hear him.

"I'm here looking for a man named John." He said loud enough to be heard over the noise.

"Tomm?" John said from inside the crowd. "Tomm is that really you?"

John stood and made his way to Tomm through the crowd.

"Oh my sweet Tomm I have longed for you." John sobbed. "I have wished for you."

John was thin and underfed but much better for wear than many of the prisoners who were quite ill. John had a secret now though. He was a God. He intended to keep it a secret.

Their embrace was long and tight. They kissed each other roughly as family does when reunited.

"My John, I was worried she had killed you."

"Not me love, not that she didn't try though."

"I as well love, and she did try." Tomm said. "I have a scar to prove it too." Tomm rubbed his cheek where the Suzy Q stood out through his trimmed beard.

"John? What do you know about these?" Tomm asked pointing to his Glow Bug.

"I invented it to save you from her." John said. "But I only made one. Now there are so many more."

"They split into two when the person they are attached to has sex." Tomm explained.

"Ahhh." John understood.

"How much can you tell me about them?" Tomm asked.

"They will protect you from any threat made against you even if it is from far away or indirect. They read the mind not only of the individual but are linked to the connected human mind.

I discovered this connection a while
back. It isn't dissimilar from the
structure of ant colonies and how they
communicate. If someone wanted to
detonate a bomb in the near vicinity
the bug would still stop it."

"Could you explain to the men what
they are?"

"I will try." John promised.

While Tomm and John were talking the
other men had also taken the
opportunity to call out for their lost
lovers if they hadn't already found
them during the release, shower and
dinner.

There was a great deal of noise now
and in John's current state it would be
very hard to get everyone's attention.

John stood on top of the table and
began.

"Your attentions please Gentlemen."
John shouted.

"Gentlemen, please. You have
questions that need answers. Some quiet
please." Tomm added when the crowd
didn't settle.

A hush fell over the room as the
other men who had joined Tomm in his
crusade motioned the men throughout the
room to quiet.

"We are all here for one reason!"
John began. "We are men who love other
men and the world president, Sue,
doesn't like gay's. She doesn't like

anyone who disagrees with her on any of her very tilted opinions."

There was a nodding of heads. All of the men had heard as much during their tortured stay here.

"This man here is my husband." John said motioning to Tomm. "The man who came here to save us is my husband, but the tool he came with which had the power to get him this far was a gift from me. It is the glowing bug flying above him, and I am its inventor."

There was a rumble through the crowd as the men began asking questions and talking to each other.

"Quiet, please gentlemen. I will explain but you need to remain quiet until I am finished."

The men quieted once again.

"The world president, Sue, has done this to us, but I have unwittingly been party to it. My name is Juan Antonio. I am her ex husband and the father of our son."

An angry rumble passed through the crowd.

"Please, gentlemen, I will tell all but hear me out before you pass judgment."

"Let the man speak!" Someone in the back of the crowd with a particularly loud voice yelled. Once again the crowd fell silent.

"I am an inventor." John began.
"Years ago in an attempt to keep my son
from wearing through his jeans at the
knees so quickly I invented a cloth
that is damn near indestructible. Most
of you have used it or purchased it at
some point before the government, Sue,
stole it from me and used it to make an
unconquerable army. This isn't all
though. Once, while in a horrible state
of jealousy, I invented a watcher to
spy on Tomm to see if he was stepping
out on me. This also she used to her
advantage. With it she made and
compiled a black list in order to find
us all and many others who aren't gay,
but were involved in other lifestyles
she didn't agree with. She kidnapped my
husband then and kept him hostage from
me for years, to blackmail me and
manipulate me. When it didn't work she
took away my son and threatened Tomm's
life. It was then that I made the first
Glow Bug to protect him. The man I
love. It is a device designed as a
bodyguard through the reading of
biology and minds of those threatening
its charge. You have all witnessed the
strength of it."

John pointed at the guards who were
almost all now awake, but who remained
gagged and tied.

"I only made one, but like my other
inventions I made it with the ability

to self replicate. I will let Tomm
explain the how."

The room was dead silent as Tomm
took the crowds attention. Standing on
a table, he looked magnificent, like a
dream of a Grecian God he stood, his
shirt unbuttoned halfway down and his
hairy chest bulging through. His
muscular, thick forearms covered with
veins. All eyes were fixed on him.

"My friends." He began. "My
brothers. I know little of the how, but
I can tell you that anyone who attempts
to hurt a man who is accompanied by a
glow bug is stopped and suffers what
appears to be the equal in pain to what
they intended for their victim."

Tomm stopped for a moment to breath
and look the crowd over.

"The point I'm trying to get to is
the way they self replicate. I didn't
know they could replicate until I had
sex with another man. He is here with
us. His name is Jim Beau." Tomm pointed
at his friend. "After we made love we
discovered that he too had a glow bug,
and likewise was safe from attacks.
Later I found out that he too had a
lover who had been taken here, to this
God forsaken place. He appears to have
found his man." Tomm noted the two
holding hands. Jim Beau looked worried
about the condition his man was in but
raised their joined hands above their

heads. The room gave a short moment of cheers, feeling exited now.

"So we have reached the point of his speech. Glow bugs will only replicate during the act of human lovemaking. When we share that connection with each other the glow bug becomes two and the new ones attach to their new charges."

Tomm paused again allowing a second for what he had said to sink in. Allowing the men a moment to speak before the crowd fell silent on their own.

"Sue must be stopped!" He then shouted as heart felt as he could. He was shaking from the hurt she had caused and the emotion of it.

"We can stop her! To start this process we must do the thing that set us apart and landed us here in this death camp, the thing that she hates, the thing she put us here to rid the world of. We must make love to one another!"

A ripple of excitement was heard running through the crowd.

"There are only thirty or so of us who came here with this blessed invention to guard us. We must share it! From this thirty we must make thousands! By morning, a glow bug must accompany all of you men, who are in good enough condition to make love. Those who are not in good enough health must in their time seek one for themselves. Most important, and finally, all of us afterward have a responsibility to diligently share them with all willing men who live."

The rumble of the crowd began again and before it got too loud to speak above Tomm raised his voice again.

"I am dirty as are my men. I invite you John to accompany me and to make love with me here among these men. I will share with you my protector and with any man who wants one until my strength is spent!"

The voices of the men would not be quieted this time and Tomm knew it so he yelled the last bit of his speech over their heads.

"To the showers men! Fuck em all!!!"

His thirty men took up the battle cry, and the freed prisoners of the camp took it up as well in their excitement.

"Fuck em all!!!"
"Fuck em all!!!"
"Fuck em all!!!"

Tomm got off of the table and embraced John.

"Let's start a revolution." He whispered into John's ear "Besides you could use another shower."

Amidst the cheers of thousands of men Tomm took John by the hand and headed to the showers.

"You sure your up for this?" John asked Tomm.

"I'm gonna cum as many times as I can before morning. I hope it will be enough."

```
Here ends book one of the Spirit Gates
              Chronicles,
            White City.
Watch for book two of the Spirit Gates
              Chronicles,
       Labyrinth of the Undead.
```

Glossary

Dry Showers: rooms for washing that
clean without the use of soap or water.
They also can heal people on a
molecular level but healing is specific
to one family's genetic markers.

Cleaners: break down all forms
nonliving organic substance within
White City. Also referred to as
builders as they were used to build the
White City

Glow Bugs: White when belonging to
innocents or undecided, blue when the
individual likes women, pink when the
individual likes men, for many
individuals the color will change as
they looked from person to person as it
read their desire of the moment. Glow
bugs appeared during the holocaust
starting in death camps. No one knows
from where the bugs originate but they
defend the person they attach to from
malicious harm. The only two ways to
get one attached to you is through
sexual intercourse or to be born from a
parent who already has one. They also
defend themselves from capture or
study. They work through chemical mind
reading and nerve manipulation making
the aggressor feel the equivalent of
the pain he wanted to cause accompanied

by paralysis. The paralysis could last for weeks if the aggressor refuses to stop the attempted violent act.

Watchers: With the appearance of small white crabs they spy on the population and transmit their audio and visual images to their counterparts the viewers.

Viewers: Similar in appearance to the watcher but much larger the viewer attaches itself to walls randomly and moves randomly showing all images that a watcher transmits to it. By audio command viewers can retrieve and show any information saved in their communal database and can get current data from any geographic location.

www.ingramcontent.com/pod-product-compliance
Lightning Source LLC
Chambersburg PA
CBHW060342030726
47497CB00003B/567

* 9 780615 253589 *